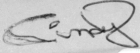

Praise f

"Kudos to Valerie Ha[...]
story with a puzzle t[...]
—RT Book Rev[...]

"Provides heart-pounding action
and heartwarming romance."
—RT Book Reviews on *The Danger Within*

"Valerie Hansen's story offers a heartwarming romance
with enough suspense to keep the pages turning."
—RT Book Reviews on *Out of the Depths*

Praise for Lynette Eason

"A beautiful mystery and a solid romance.
I highly recommend this book."
—Dee Henderson, bestselling author of the
O'Malley Family series, on *Lethal Deception*

"Lynette Eason does a fantastic job. Don't miss it."
—RT Book Reviews on *Holiday Illusion*

"A wonderful mystery."
—RT Book Reviews on *A Silent Terror*

VALERIE HANSEN

was thirty when she awoke to the presence of the Lord in her life and turned to Jesus. In the years that followed she worked with young children, both in church and secular environments. She also raised a family of her own and played foster mother to a wide assortment of furred and feathered critters.

Married to her high-school sweetheart since age seventeen, she now lives in an old farmhouse she and her husband renovated with their own hands. She loves to hike the wooded hills behind the house and reflect on the marvelous turn her life has taken. Not only is she privileged to reside among the loving, accepting folks in the breathtakingly beautiful Ozark mountains of Arkansas, she also gets to share her personal faith by telling the stories of her heart for all of Steeple Hill's Love Inspired lines.

Life doesn't get much better than that!

LYNETTE EASON

grew up in Greenville, SC. Her home church, Northgate Baptist, had a tremendous influence on her during her early years. She credits Christian parents and dedicated Sunday School teachers for her acceptance of Christ at the tender age of eight. Even as a young girl, she knew she wanted her life to reflect the love of Jesus.

Lynette attended The University of South Carolina in Columbia, then moved to Spartanburg, SC, to attend Converse College, where she obtained her master's degree in education. During this time, she met the boy next door, Jack Eason—and married him. Jack is the executive director of the Sound of Light Ministries. Lynette and Jack have two precious children, eight-year-old Lauryn, and Will, who is six. She and Jack are members of New Life Baptist Fellowship Church in Boiling Springs, SC, where Jack serves as the worship leader and Lynette teaches Sunday School to the four- and five-year-olds.

VALERIE HANSEN
LYNETTE EASON

Steeple
Hill®

Published by Steeple Hill Books™

STEEPLE HILL BOOKS

Steeple
Hill®

Recycling programs
for this product may
not exist in your area.

ISBN-13: 978-0-373-44382-6

MY DEADLY VALENTINE

Copyright © 2010 by Harlequin Books S.A.

The publisher acknowledges the copyright holders of the individual works as follows:

DANGEROUS ADMIRER
Copyright © 2010 by Valerie Whisenand

DARK OBSESSION
Copyright © 2010 by Lynette Eason

www.SteepleHill.com

Printed in U.S.A.

CONTENTS

DANGEROUS ADMIRER
Valerie Hansen

Special thanks to Sheree and Sonja, who helped me understand how a card and gift shop is run— and who also keep me well supplied with lovely merchandise. Their store is one of my very favorite places to shop.

I sought the Lord and He answered me;
He delivered me from all my fears.
—*Psalms* 34:4

PROLOGUE

I sought the Lord, and He answered me;
He delivered me from all my fears.
                              —*Psalms* 34:4

She can't do this to me. Who does she think she is?

Pacing, watching, he grew angrier as the moments passed. "Women are evil," he muttered. "They're all the same."

He stared at his hands. They weren't trembling the way they had been when he'd first realized what was really going on. Facing the problem had helped. So had making plans and looking toward the future.

Was victory going to come easily? Probably not. But he was going to enjoy every moment of the process and see it through to the end.

That conclusion made him smile. He was clever. The woman wouldn't have a clue what was going on until it was too late. And then he'd even the score. With pleasure.

ONE

"There's no holiday I like better than Valentine's Day," Rachel Hollister said. She smiled as she straightened the rack of new cards and admired the predominance of red hearts and white lace. "Except maybe for Christmas and Easter and St. Patrick's Day and…"

Eloise McCafferty, the elderly founder of the shop, chuckled. "You love greeting cards, period, Rachel. That's one of the reasons why I decided to turn this operation over to you. My dear Delbert would be rolling over in his grave if he could see how far in debt we are." She suddenly got an impish grin on her round, full face and her eyes twinkled. "Will you have to fire me to cut corners?"

"Of course not." Rachel's blue-eyed gaze met the older woman's and she realized Eloise had been teasing, although there was an element of truth to the supposition.

"Whew! That's a relief."

Sobering, Rachel patted her mentor's shoulder. "I still wish you'd let me buy an interest the way I offered to. I have a little money saved and…"

"No. You're like a daughter to me. Just don't bury yourself in this place 24/7 and miss out on the rest of life." She winked. "Like maybe marriage."

Rachel gave a nervous tug on the hem of her embroidered T-shirt and smoothed it over her jeans. "Believe me, I discovered a long time ago that I don't need a man in my life to make it whole."

"Maybe not a snob like Lance Beech or the guys you dated before he came along, but there must be a perfect husband for you somewhere."

"In a little town like Serenity? I can't see any good prospects. Besides, I prefer to stand on my own two feet."

She purposely changed the subject. "So, are you ready to tackle the last of the shipment that came in yesterday or do you want me to do it?"

"You're the boss. You tell me to jump and all I'll ask is how high."

Thoroughly enjoying the banter, Rachel nodded and pointed. "Okay, Miss Froggy. You go in the back room and check packing slips while I rearrange these drawers. There's a lot of old stock in here that I need to weed out and I wouldn't want you to feel bad having to watch."

"I don't mind as long as we donate the rejects to charity the way we planned."

"Absolutely."

Rachel pulled an empty cardboard box closer and went to work as soon as the older woman left the room. It was a tedious chore, one that muted her senses and lulled her usually quick mind into a daydreaming state.

Valentine's Day. What a lovely occasion, she mused. *Except that I rarely receive any of the sweet, sentimental cards we sell.*

Perhaps that should have bothered her but it didn't. After her recent, messy breakup with Lance and the way some of their mutual friends had started practically shunning her, even at church, Rachel was far from ready to open her heart to another man, let alone anyone local.

She was just rising and getting ready to drag the half-full cardboard box to the next drawer when she heard a muffled, squeaky noise coming from the back room.

"Eloise?"

No one answered. "Eloise? Are you all right?"

Waiting quietly for an answer and hearing nothing, Rachel frowned. That was strange. Unless Mrs. McCafferty's hearing aid battery was going dead, she should have replied.

"Eloise? Answer me."

Instead of a spoken response, Rachel heard a piercing scream! She gasped. Her feet felt rooted to the carpet. In the few seconds it took for her to force herself to move, the wordless screeching was repeated so many times she lost count.

Jace Morgan was cruising Main Street, just passing the grocery store, when the call came over his radio. He was still learning his way around the area and might have had trouble locating a residence on one of the many unmarked, outlying, dirt roads, but the commercial district was easy to navigate, especially since the sheriff's office was right across the square.

He radioed that he was on scene as he parked his black-and-white patrol car in front of the group of stores. Leaving the light bar flashing, he stepped out of the vehicle.

An icy wind chilled him through his brown bomber jacket and he shivered, reminded that he was no longer in Southern California. The streets seemed awfully quiet for a Friday morning. Then again, what did he know? Maybe for Serenity, this was bustling activity.

One thing was certain. He was a lot less likely to get shot at again while he was working this beat. The wound in his shoulder had healed nicely. The trauma of watching his partner fall remained. He still ducked when he heard loud sounds, as if facing mortal danger.

That was one of the reasons he'd left Los Angeles and had accepted an enormous cut in pay to work here. His doctors had warned him to either make some changes or risk burning out. Being a cop was in his blood. He'd never willingly stop standing for what was right in a world where so much was wrong, so he'd accepted the first job offer he'd received and here he was—in the Arkansas Ozarks—freezing to death and hoping for an early spring.

He shouldered through the front door of the card shop, fully expecting to be greeted. No one came forward. He called, "Sheriff," and paused, wary.

At the rear of the store, he heard what sounded like an argument. Releasing the safety strap on his holster, he placed his palm on the butt of his gun and waited, straining to listen.

"You did what?" came a woman's voice that sounded more than a little peeved. "What did you do *that* for?"

Jace couldn't hear the soft reply but since no one was screaming or cursing or hollering threats, he figured he'd be able to handle the situation with calming words and a logical approach.

Heading toward the origin of the conversation, he soon found himself face-to-face with two women. One was familiar because he'd introduced himself to many of the shopkeepers when he'd first been hired by Sheriff Allgood.

The other, much younger woman was new to him, and was undoubtedly the prettiest girl he'd seen in ages, with long, light brown, wavy hair and just enough freckles to make her look sun-kissed. She didn't look a bit pleased by his arrival, though. Her blue eyes narrowed and her lips pressed into a thin line. If anyone else had stared at him that way, he'd have been worried. On her, however, everything was attractive, even a frown.

Jace touched the brim of his cap and nodded politely. "One of you ladies reported a disturbance?"

"I did," the sixtyish, shorter woman answered. "I thought somebody should and Rachel wasn't about to do it."

He looked to Rachel. "Pleased to meet you, miss. How can I be of service?"

"This really isn't necessary," she argued. "Somebody is just playing a bad joke."

"Maybe you should let me decide that," Jace said. He could tell by the way she kept stepping between him and an open carton on the floor that she didn't want him to look at it. "The problem is in that box, right?"

"Yes, but…"

Deftly angling around her, he nudged the box with the toe of his boot. Bits of Styrofoam packing material were scattered across the bare floor and he could see the top of what looked like a bedraggled flower arrangement peeking through the snowy drifts left in the carton.

Scowling, Jace looked back at the women. "That bouquet must have been in transit a long time—long enough to wilt and die. That's hardly a police matter."

"I know," Rachel replied tersely. "That's what I told Eloise—Mrs. McCafferty. But she phoned the sheriff's office anyway."

He did his best to keep from sounding judgmental as he cautioned them. "Next time, I suggest you call your freight company or whoever delivered that in the first place."

"What an excellent idea," Rachel said.

Jace could tell she was mocking him but he let it slide. He needed to make friends here, not alienate the very folks he'd sworn to serve and defend.

"We can't," the older woman piped up. "That's what I've been trying to explain. Nobody's listening."

"Ma'am?"

"There's no shipping label on this box. Not even a return address. I don't know how it got back here but it didn't come in any of the usual ways."

"Are you sure?" Jace could tell by the surprised expression on the younger woman's face that this was the first she'd heard of the discrepancy. He watched her bend over, pluck a crumpled piece of paper from the carton and smooth it so she could read what was written on it.

Her eyes widened.

Jace relieved her of the note, taking care to handle it by pinching only one corner. The scrawled message made his heartbeat jump. It said,

Like my favorite girl. Once beautiful, now dead.

* * *

Rachel knew it wasn't logical to be frightened by such a silly threat but it was still upsetting. "I'm going to have nightmares for weeks," she muttered. "I know I am."

Her brow knit as she addressed the deputy. "Something else just occurred to me. If that horrible thing wasn't delivered in the regular way, how did it get into our storeroom?"

"Do you keep the back door locked?"

"We will from now on."

"How about an alarm system? Do you have one of those?"

"No." She smiled at Mrs. McCafferty. "And we can't afford to install one. We'll be fortunate to keep our doors open if we don't start to generate more sales. Which reminds me…" She briefly glanced over the officer's shoulder, then concentrated on him. "More than one of my regular customers has peered in the window since you got here. Would you mind moving that car and shutting off your flashing lights? You're bad for business."

"Will you be okay if I leave long enough to do that?"

"Of course. Why wouldn't we be?"

"Just didn't want to be accused of dereliction of duty."

Rachel huffed and peered at his name tag. "Look, Deputy Morgan, I can take care of myself and Eloise just fine. We didn't need you here in the first place."

The moment she spoke she was penitent. "I'm sorry. I didn't mean to sound so harsh. I know you're only doing your job."

"You don't care much for police officers, do you? May I ask why?"

"Well, not because I'm a crook, if that's what you're thinking," Rachel replied. "Actually, my father is a cop. Or he was, until he retired recently."

"I take it you and he don't see eye to eye." Jace's brows arched.

She laughed wryly. "That, Deputy, has to be the understatement of the century."

TWO

Jace wasn't too concerned about the strange package at the card store. After all, it hadn't been physically damaging, nor did it show much imagination. Anybody could send dead flowers as a sick joke. Considering the kinds of heinous criminal acts he'd faced in L.A., this one was little more than a nuisance.

His thoughts carried him back to the look on Rachel's face when she'd read that cryptic note. There had been an unguarded moment of fear before she'd carefully schooled her features to appear less concerned.

What was she hiding? And why? Surely she couldn't be involved in anything serious. According to Sheriff Allgood, there was little crime in Serenity and what there was, was quickly dealt with. There had only been one murder in the past three years and that crime had been solved, which told Jace that the town was about as peaceful as anyone could hope for.

He shivered. Images of his last gun battle, the one that had changed his life, flashed into his mind. He and his partner, Roy, had been patrolling an alley behind a hotel when Roy had informed him that he was going to marry the woman Jace had courted for nearly a year. Shocked and saddened, Jace had not been at his best when shots had whistled over their heads moments later.

"Duck!" Roy had shouted, grabbing his arm and dragging him behind a trash bin.

Jace crouched instinctively and drew his gun. "Where did that come from?"

"I don't know. Second story, I think. Keep your head down and cover me. I'll go around and come in the back."

Nodding, Jace tightened his grip on his pistol. His head was spinning. All he could think about was Sandra. With Roy. As a couple. And he was left out in the cold.

More shots echoed between the tall buildings. Jace tensed, looking for the source and preparing to return fire. *There. Third window from the corner.* He raise his arm and aimed.

Just then, another shooter entered the scene. Roy fell. And Jace froze, incredulous, for what seemed like an eternity. It was long enough for him to be wounded, too.

Later, when his shoulder had been bandaged and his partner had regained consciousness in the hospital, with Sandra holding his hand and weeping over him, Roy had assured Jace that there was nothing Jace could have done to prevent their injuries.

Jace hadn't been sure then and he was no more positive now. Still, the incident had served a purpose. It had demonstrated without a doubt that Sandra loved Roy. And it had given Jace a reason to change jobs, to simplify his life as well as move across the country to escape constant reminders of his lost love.

He paused in the street and glanced back at the card shop. If he were looking for a new relationship, he'd certainly be interested in getting to know Rachel better.

Good thing for him he was cured of any romantic tendencies, he thought cynically as he turned away, because that was one attractive lady.

The last thing Rachel wanted to do was report more problems to the sheriff. Unfortunately, it looked as if she was going to have to do exactly that. When she went to hang up her jacket and check the security of her back door the next morning, she found pry marks on the frame, the lock sprung and the door sagging open on damaged hinges.

"This is getting disgusting," she muttered, grabbing her cell phone.

A male voice answered, "Sheriff's office. What's your emergency?"

"This is Rachel Hollister. The back door of my store has been forced open."

"Where are you now?"

"Standing here, looking at it. Why?"

"Don't go inside. Whoever's responsible may still be there."

That had not occurred to her. "Too late. I'm already inside."

"Well get out. Now. We'll send a man right over. And stay on the line with me if you can. Are you on a cell or a landline?"

The command to remain connected hardly registered. She ended the call automatically as she gaped at the damaged door. Suddenly, the atmosphere in the storeroom seemed ice-cold in spite of the fact that she had worn a short-sleeve sweater to work instead of a blouse or T-shirt.

"That's because it's only thirty degrees outside and that broken door is open," she assured herself, rubbing her prickling forearms.

She supposed she should just step away from there, although she had already traversed the entire length of the store, turning on lights and preparing for the day's business, so what would be the point of running away? And from what? Boogeymen? Invisible adversaries?

"If there was a burglar in the shop, I sure didn't see him," she murmured.

A tremor raced up her spine and ended by needling the fine hairs on the nape of her neck. "But maybe he saw me."

That was all the incentive she needed to get moving. Rushing out into the alley, she didn't look behind her until she had reached the street in front of the store.

A patrol car was already pulling up to the curb. She was certain that the same good-looking officer as before was driving. He pretty much had to be unless Harlan Allgood, the sheriff, had decided to handle the call himself. She hadn't cared for Boyd, Harlan's previous deputy, because she'd considered him lazy and inept. This one, however, seemed far too gung ho. Judging by the way he was behaving as he got out of the car, he must be expecting to face public enemy number one!

He motioned her out of the way. His brow was knit and his eyes narrowed. He drew his gun, holding it at the ready and never taking his eyes off the storefront. Considering his formidable presence and keen concentration on the task at hand, Rachel was very glad she was one of the good guys.

Pausing at the door before pushing it open, Jace asked over his shoulder, "What did you see, exactly?"

"Just that the back door had been jimmied." She held her arms tightly against the cold—and against the thought that some criminal was targeting the poor little card shop.

"Nobody inside?"

"Not that I saw. I came all the way through…"

His brows arched. "You did *what?*"

"The same thing I do every day. I unlocked the front door, turned on the lights and went to leave my purse and coat in the back room. That's when I saw the damage and called the sheriff."

"And you left by that back door?"

"Yes."

"Well, that was *one* smart move, at least."

"Hey, if they'd posted a sign on the door that they were busy robbing the place, I'd have stayed outside," she snapped in reaction to his critical tone. "When you catch the folks who are doing this stuff, warn them to be more courteous in the future, will you?"

"Sorry. You're right. I just don't want to see anyone get hurt."

"Neither do I. I want peace and quiet. Think you can help with that?"

"I hope so. Stay here while I go check inside. When I'm finished, I'll come back for you and we'll walk through it again, together, so you can see if anything has been moved or stolen."

"Okay. Whatever you say." She noted that he seemed relieved by her quick agreement. The worrisome part of their conversation was his implication that she might have been in the actual presence of one or more thieves while innocently opening the store.

That notion gave her the shivers even more than the cold morning temperature and damp air and she hugged herself tightly. It was as if the eyes of a thousand enemies were upon her. Watching. Menacing. Waiting for her to relax and let down her guard so they could pounce.

Nervous beyond logic, she glanced up and down the familiar street. Nobody strange was hanging around as far as she could tell. There was the usual early activity in and out of the bakery as folks grabbed a quick cup of coffee and pastry. Someone was delivering that day's newspapers to the rack across the square. And the regular maintenance man was using a noisy leaf blower to clear dried leaves off the sidewalk and out of the flower beds around the courthouse. All in all, it just looked like another peaceful day in paradise.

The frightening thing was Rachel's certainty that tranquility was nothing more than an illusion.

As Jace made his way slowly up and down the aisles of the small shop, he kept his gun in hand. He doubted the perpetrators were still there but as long as there was a slight chance, he planned to be ready.

Finally satisfied that all was well, he holstered the weapon, returned to Rachel and pushed open the door. "You can come in now. There's no sign of whoever broke in."

"Are you sure?"

"Positive. You'll have to get a locksmith to repair that back door today though. I couldn't make it catch."

"Okay. What now?"

He stepped aside for her to pass. "Now, we go over the store bit by bit and you tell me if anything is missing or damaged."

"Okay. Give me a second to grab my coat from the back room, will you? I'm freezing."

Accompanying her, he stayed close, just in case. When they reached the storeroom she stopped so abruptly he almost bumped into her. "What's the matter?"

Rachel pointed. Her hand was shaking. "My—my jacket," she said in a near whisper. "I always hang it right there on that hook."

"I don't see any coat," Jace said, scowling and peering at the spot in the corner she was indicating.

"That's what I mean," she replied. "It's gone. You know what that tells us?"

"Yes." Nodding, he braced himself and pivoted to recheck every corner, every possible hiding place. When he saw the young woman sway slightly, he took her elbow to steady her. "Are you all right?"

"No. I'm not all right," Rachel said. "I'm terrified. They were still here when I came in. It wasn't just my imagination. They had to be watching my every move."

THREE

"Praise the Lord, Mrs. McCafferty isn't due to come to work till ten," Rachel told Jace. "Eloise isn't nearly as resilient as she pretends to be and I don't want to frighten her needlessly."

"Did she have trouble like this in the past?"

"Not that I know of." It had been Rachel's fondest hope that she could relieve her old friend and mentor of a lot of the stress she'd been dealing with lately, but troubling events like the one this morning were not going to be easy to tone down or cover up.

Another thought popped into Rachel's head and made her shudder and whisper, "Please, God, don't let Harlan tell my father what's been going on or I'll never hear the end of it."

"I beg your pardon?" Jace was scowling at her.

"I was just imagining what my dad's reaction to all this would be. Like I said before, he's the reason I don't particularly take to cops."

"That's too bad."

"Yes, I suppose it is. I know everyone is not like him. It's just a hang-up I happen to have. No offense meant."

"None taken." Jace continued to scan the dimly lit room. "Are there any more lights back here or is this the best it gets?"

"I have another bank of overheads. Just a sec. I'll turn them on."

Reaching behind a stack of unopened stock, she started to flip the switch. Her fingers brushed something fine, like a spider web, and she recoiled with a sharp intake of breath.

Jace was immediately at her side. "What is it? What's wrong?"

"A web, I think. It startled me, that's all. I was bitten by a brown recluse spider last year and it was not a pleasant experience. I had to take antibiotics for weeks."

"I don't doubt that." He shifted the top box until they could both peer at that portion of the wall. Instead of a real spider-web, they found a mass of gossamerlike threads arranged in a loose pattern across the switch plate.

Rachel leaned closer. "That looks like the stuff they make fake webs out of in the movies."

"Sure does." He was sweeping it away with the end of his baton to reveal a scrap of paper that was taped to the wall behind it.

When Rachel reached for it, he stopped her. "Don't touch that."

"Why not? You said you didn't find any fingerprints on the last note."

"No, but there's tape on this one," Jace said. "It's possible that your stalker left a print on the sticky side of that."

Rachel's eyes widened. She stared at his face. There was no sign that he was exaggerating, nor was there even a hint that he might be joking. "A *stalker?* You think that's what's going on?"

"I don't know. It just seems to me that this whole series of attacks is directed at you, rather than at the shop."

For the first time since she'd received the dead flowers the day before, she was ready to admit a possible pattern. Could he be right?

"I want to at least get close enough to read that note," she said flatly. "I won't touch it. I promise."

To her relief, the broad-shouldered officer gave ground and allowed her to step nearer to the paper, although he didn't walk away.

She leaned in past him, sensing his protective presence and surprisingly glad for it. The scrawled, printed words came into focus. She swayed when she read.

You are just like the black widow, my darling Rachel.
But I will kill you before you can kill me.

Jace took her arm and steadied her. "See what I meant? This isn't about the card shop. It's personal."

"I—I can see that now." She raised her gaze to his and was struck by the empathy there. "What can I do? What *should* I do?"

"You can start by telling me who's so mad at you that they're going to all this trouble," he said.

"I don't have a clue."

"How about ex-boyfriends?"

"I have one, Lance Beech, but he shouldn't be upset. Breaking off our relationship was as much his idea as it was mine." She paused. "He has been saying some unkind things about me to our mutual friends. You know, like sour grapes. But he'd never resort to this kind of harassment. I know he wouldn't."

"What about others?"

Rachel sensed that he was assessing her, judging her honesty. "Nobody serious. My dad keeps trying to fix me up with men of his choosing but I refuse to go out with any of them."

"Yet he keeps insisting? Why?"

She huffed in disgust. "Once my father gets it into his head that he's going to handle something his way, there's no stopping him. He's always treated me as if I was less than competent. When he learns there's a crime involved here, he'll probably camp on the doorstep of the shop and scare away what few customers I have left."

"Maybe he's just looking out for you."

"Not in my opinion. That's one of the reasons I stuck with

Lance Beech for way too long and ended up hurting his feelings when I didn't mean to. As long as Lance was in the picture, Dad backed off and let me live my own life."

"You don't like any of his choices? Maybe you just need to give a few of the guys a fair chance. You know. Get to know them."

Rachel bristled. "Now you're starting to sound just like Dad. Some of the men he's suggested recently are so unsuitable I'm beginning to wonder if he's actually trying to help or just make sure I'm single forever."

Jace chuckled, making her even more irate.

"I hardly think it's funny," she declared.

"I'm not laughing at what he's been doing, it's your reaction to it that's so hilarious."

"Ha-ha." Rachel straightened her spine and squared her shoulders. Truth to tell, if her father suggested she date any particular man, it was akin to waving a red flag in front of an angry bull. There was no way she was going to agree. Period. Why, she'd sooner date this new cop than accept any of her father's choices.

That notion made her grind her teeth. Date a cop? No way. Not in a million years. She didn't care if he was the best-looking man she'd met in ages—which he was. His occupation would never allow her to see him as anything but a clone of her father and that was enough to keep her from letting him get too close.

Although he did seem to be the current answer to her problems, that didn't mean he'd ever be anything more. She'd see to that.

Glancing back at the note taped to the wall, she shivered. She might not want to get to know this officer personally but it sure was nice to have him standing so close and ready to come to her defense. This was the second time her unknown nemesis had mentioned death. Under those circumstances she'd be a fool to purposely push away the one man who was poised and able to protect her.

Rachel managed to squeeze out a smile, realized how lopsided it was, and laughed at herself.

"That's better," Jace said. "I was wondering how long you were going to stay mad at me."

"I'm more mad at myself than I am at you," she admitted ruefully, eyeing the broken door. "I don't suppose you can hang around till I can have that repaired?"

"I'll do better than that. Get me a few tools and I'll fix it for you, at least temporarily."

"Is that allowed? I mean, you are on duty."

"I'll be securing a crime scene," he said with a grin. "Besides, there's not exactly an overabundance of trouble here in Serenity. Yours are the only real calls I've had since I came to work here."

"That's me," Rachel quipped, "a one-woman crime spree. Anything to keep the local law from getting bored."

She saw his smile fade and his eyes narrow, clearly concentrating on her as he added, "It's okay to joke about it to relieve tension, but that doesn't mean I consider these threats harmless. You do understand that, don't you?"

Nodding, she met his firm gaze with resolution. There was a knot in her stomach and a lump in her throat when she said, "Oh, yes, Deputy Morgan. I understand it all too well."

"You can call me Jace, if you want," he said as he went to work with a hammer and screwdriver. "First names seem to be the norm around here."

"For those of us who have lived here all our lives, they are. As a newcomer, you may find that some folks are a bit stand-offish."

"How long do you think it will take for them to loosen up toward me?"

Rachel laughed lightly. "Oh, two or three…"

"Months?"

"No, generations. If you stay all your life, your grandkids will probably be considered locals."

"I see."

He tried to concentrate on fixing the door but thoughts of the woman beside him kept interfering. She was spunky without being foolish, pretty without being conceited and intelligent enough to impress him beyond all expectations. That he'd even noticed was a surprise, especially since he'd sworn off women in general, beautiful ones in particular. He had his work, his career. It was his mission in life. He didn't need the distraction of a romantic entanglement. That kind of thing had almost cost him his former partner's life. He was not about to make the same mistake twice.

Still, he reasoned, if he made himself available to Rachel Hollister in his off-duty hours, he might be in a better position to solve the mystery of who was threatening her. In a close-knit community like this one, there was little chance he'd inadvertently stumble upon the information he needed to keep her safe unless he was totally immersed in the day-to-day activities.

As he worked, he kept his eyes on the door. "Where do you go to church?"

"Why?"

"Just wondered. I'm new here, as you know, and I thought I'd ask around for recommendations."

"I— Serenity Chapel is nice."

"Is that your church?" Noting her reluctance, he began to watch her, to probe her expression.

"I don't go very often. Not anymore."

Finished, Jace straightened to try the repaired door and test its strength. "Why not?"

"Because of Lance, mostly. His parents are important church members and I told you he was spreading false rumors about why we broke up, probably to save face. I started feeling uncomfortable because I could sense that so many people believed his exaggerations. They didn't say so to my face, but…"

"Don't you think you're overreacting? The way I look at

it, it may be nice to visit with friends at church but that's not the real reason to attend. We're supposed to be there to worship."

"Tell that to Lance."

"I will, if you'll accompany me to the Sunday morning service."

"Oh, I don't think…"

"Don't think. Just put on your big girl shoes and do it, as my granny used to say." He could feel himself beginning to blush. "Of course, that's not exactly how she put it but you get the general idea."

"I've heard similar old sayings right around here." Rachel frowned. "I thought you were from California."

"I am. My grandparents, however, were genuine hillbillies, just like you." He was pleased to see her smile and chuckle.

"Don't let too many folks hear you call us that," she warned. "We may refer to ourselves that way but we tend to take exception to having outsiders do it."

"I'll be careful. So, how about it? Will you go to church with me and introduce me around?" Waiting, he was afraid she'd refuse so he goaded her. "Unless these childish threats have you ready to hide from life and turn into a hermit."

"Me? Hide? No way," she insisted.

"Good. Then tell me where you live and what time you want me to pick you up Sunday morning."

"I never said I'd go."

"No," he drawled, "but you didn't say you wouldn't, either."

The look of alarm on her face was priceless. Jace hoped she could tell that his interest was purely platonic because he didn't want to create a false impression that he was actually pursuing her.

Moments later he stopped worrying. After all, how much more innocent could their time together be? He did want to find a home church and since the Good Lord had placed Rachel in his life, he figured it was only sensible to kill two birds with one stone.

That analogy immediately chilled him to the bone. Any mention of killing brought his thoughts back to the threatening notes. And to the looming danger that he had yet to identify, let alone counteract.

FOUR

Sunday morning dawned bright and sunny, although the temperature was predicted to rise no higher than forty degrees by afternoon. Rachel wasn't surprised. There were slim daffodil fronds peeking out of the ground and a few crocuses and hyacinths had already bloomed. Other than that, there was little sign that winter was past.

Shivering, she pulled her wool coat over her pale blue sweater and skirt, picked up her purse and bible and stepped out onto the front porch of her modest brick home to wait for Jace.

Chilly weather wasn't the only reason she was trembling, she realized with chagrin. Going back to church after having been absent for so many months was bound to cause a stir. So was being accompanied by a handsome newcomer.

That thought made her smile in spite of her misgivings. She knew it was wrong to gloat but she could hardly wait till the news of her arrival reached Lance Beech and his cohorts.

"Some loving Christian I am," Rachel admonished herself. "Shame on me."

Sighing, she closed her eyes and said a quick prayer for forgiveness. She and Lance had parted amiably, at least as far as she was concerned. Why he had grown so antagonistic afterward was beyond her. She had phoned several times and tried to get him to discuss their breakup but he had always hung up on her, leaving her to come to her own conclusions.

The thing that hurt the most was that so many folks had sided with him. At least that was how it had seemed. In retrospect, she wondered if her own guilty conscience about the breakup had colored her perception or made her imagine negative reactions from other people that were not really that bad.

Noticing the slow approach of a white pickup truck, Rachel's heart leaped. Was that Jace? If so, he was right on time.

She waved. The truck pulled into the circular drive and stopped in front of her. Before the driver had time to jump out, let alone circle to the passenger side, Rachel was already climbing in.

"I would have opened that door for you," he said.

"Sorry." Her tingling cheeks warmed under his scrutiny and the slanting rays of the sun. "I was in a hurry because it's so nippy out this morning."

He rubbed his hands together and blew on them, creating a cloud of steam inside the truck's cab. "I know what you mean. I didn't care that my truck's heater was broken when I lived in California. I haven't been this cold since I went to ski camp in my teens."

"I've never been skiing," Rachel said, thankful that he was making small talk rather than being too serious.

"So, how long will it be before we see summer around here? I can hardly wait."

"You won't be saying that when it's over ninety degrees with one hundred percent humidity." Rachel laughed when he made a silly face. "I'm not kidding. It gets good and hot during the middle of summer in Arkansas."

"Thanks for the warning. I'll remember that. Any other tips you can offer a California transplant?"

"Well, stay out of the long grass and weeds as soon as the temperature warms up."

"Because of snakes?"

Rachel fastened her seat belt as he pulled away from the curb and started down the road. "Them, too. But it was ticks and chiggers I was thinking of. They lie in wait in the grass and then jump onto your ankles."

"I know about ticks. What's a chigger?"

"Invisible and itchy. You'll find out soon enough. One misstep and you'll be an expert." She leaned forward and pointed. "Slow down. There's Serenity Chapel."

A sloping asphalt drive led to the church that was perched at the front of a hill. Behind it, redbud trees were showing the first flush of pink color against the dark green cedars. Many oaks stood bare, awaiting the warmth and longer days of spring as their signal to leaf out.

"Where do you want me to park?" Jace asked.

"Anywhere is fine. I'm not fussy."

She was gathering up her belongings when the cell phone in her purse jingled a tune. "Oops. I forgot to shut that off. Good thing it didn't ring during the sermon or Pastor Malloy would have been upset."

Unfolding the little phone and putting it to her ear, she smiled and offered a cheery "Hello?"

No one responded. Rachel scowled. "Hello? Is anybody there?" She held it out and looked to see if there was a number she recognized on the lighted screen. Apparently, the number had been blocked. "Huh."

"What's the matter?" Jace asked.

"There's nobody on the line. You heard the phone ring, too, didn't you?"

"Yes. Loud and clear. Maybe it was one of those computer-generated calls where they try to sell you something."

"That's probably it. Oh, well, it served a purpose. It reminded me to shut this off." Before she could do so, however, the little phone rang a second time.

"Hello? Hello?"

This time, instead of silence, Rachel heard an indistinguishable sound. "What? Speak up, please. I can't hear you."

She looked at Jace and noticed that he was on full alert, scanning the church parking lot through the truck's windows.

"Who is it?" he asked.

"I don't know."

Just then, in the temporary hush before Jace spoke again, she heard a distinctive sound. Someone was breathing hoarsely, harshly, as if bent on sounding menacing.

"I'm not afraid of you," Rachel insisted, although her hands were shaking.

Jace snatched the phone away from her and held it to his ear.

"Nothing," he said a few seconds later. "The connection's broken."

As he handed the cell phone back to her his warm, reassuring touch lingered on her hands, cupping them and stilling their quaking.

She didn't mind one bit. "It's not even safe at church," she whispered, biting back tears.

"You're safe with me," he assured her. "Wherever we are, I'll keep you safe. I promise."

"How? We don't even know who or what we're up against."

She could tell from his tight-lipped expression that he had no ready answer, no explanation that would calm her fears.

That's because he knows there's real danger, she concluded with a start. She wasn't the only one who was nervous. Her companion and protector was just as tense as she was. And that scared her even more.

In light of all that had happened, it was hard for Jace to relax and participate in the worship service because he kept looking for clues about who might have been threatening Rachel. Given the timing of the cell calls, he assumed that whoever had made them had been watching. To have done that, he would have had to be in or near the church parking lot. Therefore, he might also be taking part in the service.

By Jace's estimation there were at least a hundred men in attendance, which gave him plenty of suspects. However, just because the threatening notes were phrased as if composed by a man, that was no guarantee there was no woman involved. He'd seen plenty of cases that had seemed to be of masculine origin which had turned out otherwise.

Solving this puzzle was not going to be easy, Jace mused, shaking hands with fellow worshippers after the conclusion of the service. Rachel had introduced him to so many people he was thoroughly confused, especially when she tried to relate one to another by mentioning the participants' kinship.

Finally, he held up his hands in surrender. "Whoa. I appreciate your trying to orient me as to who's who, but you lost me at the last third-cousin-twice-removed."

Rachel chuckled. "Sorry. You'll be all right as long as you remember that nearly everyone is related in some way to everybody else."

He saw her jaw clench and noticed that she'd suddenly sobered. "What is it? Something wrong?"

"Only the usual," she said. "See that man over there in the tan sport jacket? That's my father. I had hoped we could get in and out of here without running into him, but he's seen us."

"Who's that with him?"

"One of the guys I told you about. Dad wants me to date him."

"How can I help?"

"Just be yourself." She snickered. "I think. I really don't know you well enough to be certain, but I suspect my father won't like you much. He's never approved of any of my friends."

"Then we should give him something to think about," Jace said, slipping his left arm lightly around the waist of her coat and pulling her close to his side in spite of the resistance he could feel from her as her father walked toward them. "Try to act as if you like me. We'll never fool him if you look like you're about to clobber me for getting fresh."

"Who says I'm not?"

He laughed. "Atta girl. Keep that spunky spirit and you'll

be fine." Sticking out his free hand and smiling, he preempted Mr. Hollister's anticipated criticism with a cheerful, "Glad to meet you, sir. Rachel's told me so much about you. It's a real pleasure."

Beside him, he felt the young woman's tension start to ebb, especially once her father had accepted the offer to shake hands. Although the older gentleman was scowling and so was the slim, twentysomething man with him, Jace felt as if he had won the first skirmish. He was sure it helped that their meeting had taken place right outside the church and in the presence of so many townspeople.

Rachel found her voice. "Dad, I'd like you to meet Jace Morgan. Jace, this is my father, George Hollister. And this is…"

"Alan Caldwell," the younger, dark-haired man said, also offering his hand.

"Pleased to meet you both." There was no doubt in Jace's mind that neither George nor Alan was really pleased to make his acquaintance. They were both smiling and acting amiable enough but there was an undercurrent of tension as thick as L.A. smog on a windless day.

George cleared his throat. "So, you're the new deputy Harlan hired. I'd wondered what you looked like. Should have spotted you from the military haircut."

"And now we've officially met, so you know," Jace said with a smile, then turned his eyes on Rachel and gave her a barely perceptible squeeze. "I think I'm really going to like it here."

To his surprise and amusement, she tilted her head, looked up and batted her eyelashes at him. Jace nearly burst into laughter. Whether her father took her actions seriously or not, the whole scenario was hilarious.

Apparently, Alan was not amused. The younger man wheeled and stalked off while Rachel's father blustered something about having to meet someone for Sunday dinner, then also took his leave.

As soon as George was out of sight, Jace loosened his grip and stepped away. "That was fun. I think we got his attention."

Rachel giggled. "Looks like it. I can hardly wait till he phones me and reads me the riot act about keeping company with a man who's not from around here."

"That's a prerequisite?"

"Absolutely. Dad will want to know your grandpa and father, at least, not to mention your more distant kin."

"Then he's out of luck," Jace said, still smiling. "They're both deceased."

"I'm sorry."

"Yeah, me, too. But life goes on." He led the way toward his truck. "So, what do folks do around here on a Sunday afternoon?"

"Usually go out for dinner, then kick back at home. What did you have in mind?"

Jace shrugged, hoping he looked nonchalant. "I don't know. It's getting a little warmer but I suppose it's still too cold for a picnic."

"Only if you want to avoid frostbite."

"I know what you mean. I almost gave in and wore my uniform jacket over my suit this morning. I thought this was the south. It's supposed to be hot here."

"Like I said, it will be in a few more months. It's barely February."

"I know. But I keep hoping." As Jace approached his pickup on the passenger side to unlock the door for her, he noticed what looked like a flyer tucked under one of the wiper blades. A quick perusal of nearby vehicles told him that no other cars had been similarly tagged.

He put out an arm to block her path. "Hold it. Wait here."

"Why? What's wrong?"

"Probably nothing. I just want to be sure before you get into the truck."

"Sure of what?"

Jace didn't answer. He leaned over so he could read the

note without touching it, then got down on his knees to check the vehicle's undercarriage, just in case.

When he rose and dusted himself off, he returned to Rachel. "We'll need to phone the sheriff's office."

"Why? What is it?"

"Another threat," he said, stepping between her and the few cars that remained in the lot. "I was afraid we were being watched."

Her voice quavered. "And?"

"And, unfortunately, I was right."

FIVE

The springtime sun was still shining overhead but in Rachel's heart, it was the depth of winter. This couldn't be happening to her. Not in Serenity. And surely not at church.

Pastor Logan Malloy joined the small group gathered around Jace's truck, listened to what was being said, then spoke directly to the sheriff. "Hi, Harlan. What's the trouble?"

"Just tomfoolery," the portly sheriff insisted. "Pure and simple. Some yahoo's got a grudge against Miss Rachel here and he's actin' out by leavin' threats. Last one was stuck on this here truck."

Before she could speak in her own defense, the pastor did it for her. "I wouldn't be so quick to brush it off as an innocent prank if I were you. Anybody who's willing to behave like this on church property shows no conscience. And little or no regard for right and wrong, either, assuming they're able to tell the difference."

Rachel sensed Jace's closeness and once again stepped into the shelter of his arm around her shoulders, unconcerned about social proprieties. Truthfully, she felt a lot less bashful than usual, especially since there was so much strength and comfort associated with his presence.

The fact that all the men had begun casting questioning glances at Jace convinced her that further explanations were in order. "Jace—Deputy Morgan—was the one who responded to the first threat at the shop and he's been very helpful ever since."

"You have his references?" Logan asked Harlan.

"Yep. All in order. He comes highly recommended. All the way from Los Angeles, too."

"I see."

"Really, Pastor Logan," Rachel said. "You're beginning to sound as critical as my father."

With that, the pastor smiled. "I am like a father in many ways. You're a member of my flock so that makes you partly my responsibility." He offered his hand to Jace. "Sorry if I sounded suspicious."

Jace grinned and shook his hand firmly. "No problem. I know why you did. Because I'm not from around here, right?"

"Right. We tend to look after our own. Is this your first visit to Serenity Chapel, Jace?"

"Yes. Miss Hollister invited me and I thought it would be best if she didn't drive over alone. Not till the sheriff and I get to the bottom of her troubles."

"If you have a few minutes, I'd like to discuss the case with you. That is, if Harlan doesn't mind."

The sheriff shook his head, making his jowls shimmy. "Naw. You go ahead, Pastor Malloy. I know you're just like an old fire horse. No matter how long ago you quit, being a detective is in your blood."

"That it is." Turning to Rachel, Logan Malloy said, "We can talk in my office."

"Fine. I have nothing to hide," she told him, falling into step between the pastor and Jace. "I haven't done one thing wrong."

She felt Jace's hand lightly touch hers before he said, "You may not think you have, but somebody sure does."

The realization of how right he was sank into Rachel's consciousness and gave her chills from her toes to the nape of her neck. Somebody disliked her enough to try to scare her to death with empty threats.

Suddenly, a far worse theory arose. What if the threats weren't empty? What if her antagonist meant to do her real harm?

The pastor's study reminded Jace more of a den than an office. Although there were floor-to-ceiling bookshelves along one wall and a desk in the corner, there was also a cozy seating arrangement with a sofa and several comfortable chairs.

Rachel took one of the chairs, so Jace chose the couch. He leaned back and stretched out his long legs before lacing his fingers behind his head. It wasn't until he saw Rachel's eyes widen that he realized the pose had exposed the sidearm he carried beneath his suit jacket.

He adjusted the jacket and straightened. "Sorry about that."

She was shaking her head. "I should have known. My father rarely went anywhere without a gun."

"Where did he work?" Jace asked. "Harlan acts as if he's had the sheriff's job in Serenity for ages."

"He has," Logan chimed in. "It's an elected office with very few qualifications other than a clean record and enough buddies to vote you in."

"My dad worked down in Little Rock for a while," Rachel said. "As he got older he was promoted to detective and assigned to a drug task force. That took him all over the state but he spent as much time at home as possible." She smiled wistfully. "My mother wasn't bothered a bit by his being away so much. She's always been independent."

"Like you," Jace said with a smile, noting that his comment did not seem to please Rachel as much as he'd hoped it would.

"I prefer to think of myself as unique."

"That, you are," the pastor said. "By the way, the folks at the halfway house want to thank you for all the cards and the roll of postage stamps. Most of them love to send mail but rarely have enough money to buy anything nice like that."

"You're welcome."

"So," Logan went on, "what is it that's going on in your life? Who do you suspect is harassing you?"

She shrugged. "I don't have a clue. It all started a few days ago and it's just been getting worse and worse."

If Jace had not sensed that she was fighting tears he would have stayed put. When he noticed her misty eyes, however, he got to his feet, circled her chair, and laid one hand lightly on her shoulder for moral support while he addressed their host.

"The sheriff said you were a detective?"

"In days gone by," Logan replied. He swept his arm in an arc that encompassed the room. "This is my true calling. But I do occasionally find use for some of the things I learned in my former life."

"All right," Jace said. "This is what I know personally. The first reported incident was a box of dead flowers and the cryptic note that came with it. That was Friday morning."

"How was it delivered?"

"It had to be in person. There was no shipping label and no indication that one had been removed."

"Go on."

"The second note was found Saturday after the back door was jimmied, but it could have been there all along and we simply missed seeing it."

Logan leaned his elbows on his desk and steepled his fingers. "Is that what you think?"

"No. I think it was two separate attacks. The third was the one outside here, the note on my truck this morning."

"You're forgetting the calls," Rachel said. "I got weird phone calls just before the service."

"Where were you at that time?" Logan asked.

Jace answered, "In your parking lot. I assume that whoever made the calls was watching. As soon as we went inside, he knew he'd have plenty of time to place another note without being seen."

Nodding, Logan scowled. "I agree. And, unfortunately,

we've never had a need for surveillance cameras around the church until now. I'll speak to the church council about getting some ASAP."

"There's one more thing," Jace said. "Harlan didn't seem to think it was significant, but all the notes were printed with children's crayons. I thought that was kind of odd."

"It is interesting," Logan said. "What conclusion do you draw?"

"None, so far, except maybe that the perpetrator was trying to emulate childish writing. The letters were shaky and poorly made." Jace felt Rachel's shoulder tremble beneath his touch. "The sheriff didn't even send the notes to a crime lab. He said he refused to waste his skimpy budget on such nonsense—and that's a quote."

"Censored, since we're in a church, I imagine." The pastor smiled benevolently at Rachel. "Tell you what. I still have a few contacts in law enforcement in Chicago. I'll see if Harlan will let me get the notes analyzed for him."

"Oh, thank you," Rachel said. She got to her feet and held out her hand. "Even if you don't find out anything new, at least I'll feel as if somebody else is trying to do something to help me."

Logan grasped her hand and glanced over her shoulder at Jace. When he said "I thank the Lord that you have someone like this in your corner, too," Jace felt uncharacteristically uncomfortable.

"Just doing my job," he said flatly, dismissing the compliment.

"Over and above the call of duty," Logan countered, "but have it your way. As I often say, 'The Lord works in mysterious ways.'"

"Well, it wasn't God who brought me to Serenity," Jace insisted.

"Oh? Why did you come here?"

He could have answered truthfully, simply, and ended the query. He could also have revealed details of his previous anger and the resulting inadequate job performance that had nearly cost a man's life. Instead, he chose to avoid any explanation that might touch him too deeply.

"I needed a change of scenery and this assignment seemed perfect," Jace said, feigning a nonchalance that he did not feel.

He wasn't sure if it was the preacher in Logan Malloy who saw through him or if it was the former detective who was peering all the way into his wounded soul. Either way, he didn't like feeling so exposed, so vulnerable.

Rather than remain longer and face more questions, Jace reached for Rachel's hand and gave it a tug. "If you have any ideas that might help, you can reach me at the sheriff's office or at Rachel's card shop."

"Fine. I'll start by talking to Harlan and offering those tests."

"Good. Thanks." Jace was already guiding her toward the exit. "We're going to go grab a bite to eat."

"Would you like to have prayer before you go?"

Jace would have continued out the door if Rachel had not balked. "I—I'd like that." Her gaze searched Jace's. "Would you mind?"

"Not at all." And he didn't. Not really. He had often prayed for himself and his loved ones in the past. And he'd certainly prayed for his partner's survival after the gun battle that had left them both wounded.

That prayer had been answered, although not in exactly the way Jace had envisioned. Roy had lived, all right. Lived to steal Sandra's affection for good.

Why had God allowed that to happen? Jace wondered silently as the pastor began to pray aloud. He and Sandra had seemed perfect for each other, real soul mates. Yet she had chosen another man.

Yeah, a man that I almost got killed, he mused. *But I didn't do it on purpose. I couldn't have.*

Peace descended like a blanket of warmth, draping around his tense shoulders and soothing him all the way to his core.

It wasn't just wishful thinking. He had not caused anyone harm on purpose. He suddenly knew that with great certainty.

Thank You, Father, he thought as he blinked back unshed tears. *Thank You for everything, even losing Sandra.*

The fact that he was able to pray that prayer and truly mean it spoke deep into his heart. He was genuinely thankful that he had not remained in that relationship, even though its end had caused him such anguish.

But why? he wondered. Was it all really predestination? Was there such a thing? And if so, was there more to the overall scenario, such as his landing in Serenity just when Rachel Hollister needed him?

That notion did not sit well with Jace. He was perfectly willing to believe that he and Sandra did not belong together. He was far less eager to accept the idea that he had been sent to Arkansas for the sake of one particular woman.

As Logan said "Amen," his gaze connected with Jace's and Jace felt as if the pastor could peer directly into his soul. Perhaps Logan was still not sure that Jace's motives were pure. Or maybe he was just the kind of man who sensed undercurrents of unrest.

"Call me any time you want to talk," Logan said, shaking Jace's hand firmly in parting.

"Keep us posted about the lab work," Jace said. He knew that wasn't all the pastor had meant by the offer. Logan obviously knew plenty about human nature and it wouldn't have surprised Jace to learn that he also planned to phone California to check his references, something Harlan had probably not bothered to do.

Well, so be it. Jace had nothing to hide. He might not be proud of his actions in regard to his former partner but he had been formally cleared of any wrongdoing. If those reports weren't enough to satisfy the local law enforcement folks, then he'd just move on to another job.

Only not yet, he warned himself. *Not until I see that Rachel is safe and whoever is stalking her is properly punished.*

So, where did you get the idea that she needs only you? he asked himself cynically. *Anybody could protect her.*

Except that he was the one who had evidently been put in place to do so, he added with a scowl. If this situation was God's idea of a joke, it wasn't a very funny one.

SIX

Rachel wasn't a bit hungry. Still, she went through the motions of enjoying her meal, seated with Jace in the booth at Hickory Station, rather than disappoint him. He really was good company—for a cop. That mental disqualification made her smile.

"What's so funny?"

"Me," she answered, feeling her cheeks flush.

"Is that why you're blushing?"

"I am not." But she was, and she knew it. Worse, she didn't seem to be able to stop. The more time she spent in Jace's presence, the more she felt like a teenager experiencing her first crush.

"Have another piece of pizza," Jace urged. "I can't eat all this by myself."

"Then take the leftovers home with you. Where do you live, anyway? I never asked."

"Right now, behind the jail in the old caretaker's quarters. I haven't been able to find a decent apartment."

"I'm not surprised. You'd be better off looking for a house. There aren't any apartments closer than Hardy, unless you want to live at one of the old motels, and they don't offer the same facilities as a regular house."

"I've been checking the ads in the local papers but there hasn't been a thing listed that I'd consider."

"No wonder," she said, smiling knowingly. "You're going about it all wrong. Nobody advertises the good places. They don't have to. It's all handled by word of mouth." The astonished expression on his face made her chuckle.

"Really? No ads, no nothing?"

"Nope. I suppose a real estate broker like Smith Burnett could help you but the best way is to just put out the word that you're looking and wait." She grinned across the narrow, Formica-topped table at him. "Want me to ask around for you?"

"Sure. I'm willing to consider almost any kind of place as long as it's bigger than the caretaker's rooms. I don't like hanging out at the jail all the time. I have no real off-duty time when I'm that handy."

"I understand. Sometimes I feel as if I might as well sleep at the card shop." She checked her watch. "Which reminds me. Would you mind dropping me off there? I have a few things to do that I didn't finish on Saturday."

"Then how would you get home? It's still too cold to walk and your house is at least a mile from the square."

"A mile and a quarter," Rachel said. "I don't mind walking. I love the exercise and the fresh air."

Jace shook his head. "No way am I leaving you like that. If you want to go by the shop, fine. I'll wait for you."

"Have it your way," she said, hoping that she didn't sound too happy about his decision. The last thing she wanted to do was inconvenience him, yet the notion of being the only one in the empty store and then having to walk home, unescorted, gave her the shivers.

That reaction angered and disgusted her. Someone had done this to her, had stolen her peace of mind and left her unsure of everything. It wasn't fair. It also wasn't easy to push those feelings aside and ignore them.

Perhaps her strong craving for Jace's continuing company was the Lord's way of taking care of her, she thought, slightly amused by the convenient rationalization. Nevertheless, she did want him with her and was well aware that that was the smartest move.

"I would be delighted if you stayed with me," she finally admitted. "I really don't relish spending a lot of time alone in the shop. Not when we're closed, at any rate."

His resulting grin warmed her cheeks to the point where she knew she could never deny the telling reaction. She averted her gaze and busied herself picking up her purse and grabbing her good coat off the booth bench. "Well, shall we get going?"

"As soon as I get a box for our snack later," he said.

Later? Her eyebrows arched as she watched him walk to the counter and speak to the clerk.

Yes, later, she told herself. It was evident that Jace was planning to spend the whole day with her. Why she had not realized it sooner was a tribute to her closed mind. The man had appointed himself her guardian and was not about to leave her to fend for herself.

To Rachel's surprise, she was not only in total agreement, she was thrilled.

Chalk up another point for my stalker, she thought, sighing and shaking her head. *In less than a week my whole outlook has changed and I don't like it. I don't like it one little bit.*

Jace wasn't too concerned about Rachel's safety as long as they were together but he sure wasn't looking forward to the moment when he had to bid her goodbye.

One problem at a time, he lectured himself. As the Good Book said, "The cares of the day are sufficient."

Pulling to a stop in front of the card store, he asked, "Is this okay? I won't be taking up customer parking on a Sunday."

"It's fine." Her smile warmed his heart. "Being such a recent transplant, I'm surprised you remembered that most places close on the Sabbath."

"How could I forget? I figure we were fortunate to find a decent place to eat."

"The grocery mart used to be closed Sunday mornings," Rachel told him as he escorted her from the truck. "Lately, though, more and more businesses are staying open seven days a week. I'm kind of sorry to see that happening."

"You have no plans to do it, do you?"

"Absolutely not. I think it sets a bad example. Besides, even store managers need a little time off. I want my day of rest." She put the key in the lock and turned it.

Jace laughed. "Oh, really? Then why are we here?"

"I'm resting. As long as I don't have to deal with customers, it's not stressful."

"Selling cards and gifts is stressful?" He held the door for her so she could pass through ahead of him.

"It can be." She stopped in the doorway, almost causing him to bump into her as he followed. "Good grief."

"What's wrong?"

"Don't you feel it? It must be a hundred degrees in here."

He took a deep breath to test the air. "You're right. I don't smell any smoke, though. Maybe your furnace is malfunctioning."

"Maybe."

Dogging her steps, he followed her to the control panel. All the electrical fuses were in order but there were exposed wires where the power fed into the thermostat that controlled heating and cooling.

Rachel pointed. "Look."

"I see it." Every muscle in Jace's body was tensed for defense and his hand hovered near his hidden holster. "I want you to go wait outside while I look this place over thoroughly."

"No way, mister. This store is half mine and I'm not going to let anybody chase me off."

He figured it was just as well to keep her with him so he relented. "Okay. But stay behind me and don't argue."

"Me? I never argue with you."

"Right."

"Well, hardly ever. Is there any way we can shut off this heat before we go any farther? I'm roasting and it's terrible for all my decorative candles. They may already be ruined."

"I'm no electrician. If we mess with this, we may not only destroy clues, we may trigger something else much worse than a little heat."

He hated to be so blunt but he didn't want her taking matters into her own hands and getting hurt. Or worse. Judging by the look on her face she was taking his warnings very seriously.

"You mean like a *bomb?*"

"I don't know. And neither do you, so I suggest you not touch anything."

"Yes, sir. You're the boss."

Satisfied, he drew his pistol and led her slowly toward the back room, fully expecting to see that that was how the intruder had gained access again. To his shock, the heavy metal rear door was securely in place this time.

As soon as he had poked into every corner and closet, he holstered his gun. "Okay. We're alone. So, tell me, how many people have keys to this store?"

"Just me and Eloise, as far as I know. I suppose she may have more than one set but I have only the one that she gave me when she made me the manager."

"What, exactly, is your job here?"

"I run the place," Rachel said. "Eloise has been having some health problems and she's really not good at making decisions. Her late husband, Delbert, used to handle the mechanics of the store while she waited on customers. Since he's been gone, business has really been poor. When she offered me a partnership, I couldn't refuse."

"You invested?"

Rachel shook her head. "No. I wanted to. But she insisted that I was like family to her and we became partners without any money changing hands. I didn't like the idea. Still don't."

"She has no blood relatives?"

"There is a nephew. Her sister's grown son. He pitched a fit when Eloise told him what she planned to do. He actually threatened to file papers alleging she was senile."

That was the most interesting thing Jace had heard since the beginning of this apparent vendetta. "Really. Hmm. What else do you know about him? Is he local?"

"No. He lives in Tennessee, near Memphis. Why? Surely you don't think he'd go to all this trouble to scare me off. What would he gain?"

"The business, for starters." To his chagrin, Rachel laughed.

"If he had any idea how little this store is worth, he'd run for the hills. Considering all the money we still owe our suppliers, we'd be lucky to break even, let alone make a profit, even if we sold out to the bare walls."

"Then somebody should tell the guy. I will, if you or Mrs. McCafferty don't want to do it."

"Eloise has already tried. He didn't believe her. I get the idea he's not the most open-minded person."

"Get me his name and phone number. I'll take care of it."

"No."

He scowled at her. "Why not?"

"Because, the problem is between Mrs. McCafferty and her relative. Neither of us should interfere. It wouldn't be right."

"And this kind of harassment *is?*" Swinging his arm in a broad arc, Jace indicated the whole shop.

"If he's guilty, no. But you're just guessing. He may be totally innocent and you'd be accusing the wrong man."

Although he hated to admit it, she did have a valid point. "All right. Just tell me his name and let me look into his background. Surely, that won't hurt. And in the meantime, you're not to come here again unless someone is with you."

"Like who? Like you? What're you going to do, volunteer to work for me?"

"If necessary."

"Don't be ridiculous. You have a real job. Harlan would have your hide if you spent all your time over here."

Nodding, Jace had to agree. "That reminds me. We need to call the sheriff and report this as another break-in."

"How? Both doors are secure and there's no other access."

"Then you need to change the locks. I'll do that for you today, before we leave." To his disappointment, Rachel began to laugh. "What's so funny? This is serious."

"I know it is. The hilarious part is you, thinking you can buy new hardware on a Sunday. Here we sit, smack-dab in the middle of the Bible Belt, and the guy from California thinks he can actually find a place around here that will sell him anything other than a loaf of bread or a carton of milk on the Sabbath."

"Then you and I are getting out of here right now," Jace insisted. "Whether you like it or not."

"Suppose I don't want to go?"

In his heart he knew she was bluffing. He also knew that she was prejudiced against the kind of strong-arm tactics and coercion her father had employed.

At this point in their tenuous relationship, Jace figured he could either alienate her by using force or possibly set her against him even more by trying something a lot more drastic. He opted for the latter because it appealed to him on a personal level.

Reaching for her, he swept her into his embrace. The moment she raised her face to protest, he silenced her with a quick kiss.

Because he had expected her to resist, he had not been prepared for what actually happened. Rachel practically melted in his arms. Her eyes grew misty. Her lips trembled. And Jace received the sweetest, most poignant kiss of his lifetime.

If anyone had told him what it would be like to kiss her, he would not have believed them. He was standing there, experiencing it for himself, yet he could barely accept the truth.

Worse, he knew that he had not only overstepped the bounds of propriety, he had just experienced a kiss that he would remember for the rest of his life.

He was in deep, deep trouble.

SEVEN

Rachel could barely breathe, and it wasn't because the shop was stuffy enough to melt candles. Eyes wide, she managed a soft "Whew!"

To her chagrin, Jace pushed her away. "Yeah. You can say that again."

"Okay. Whew. What just happened, anyway?"

"I got stupid," he said with a wry grimace. "Sorry."

"Me, too." She giggled. "Sorry, I mean, not stupid. You caught me by surprise."

"And you handled it very well, if I do say so," he gibed. "I promise it won't happen again."

She wasn't sure she liked that vow but she was loath to admit it, even to herself. "Okay. In that case, I guess you're forgiven. What were you trying to do, convince me to leave with you?"

Watching his expression, Rachel was certain he was beginning to look relieved. When he nodded and said, "Yeah, that was it," she was convinced that he was being at least partially truthful.

"Okay," she said, chin held high. "You want us to leave, we'll leave. We can use my cell to call Harlan. But I'm not going home until I get the heat turned off in here. I won't be responsible for having everything ruined when I could have stopped it. Besides, with the wiring so exposed there might be a fire."

"I suppose you're right," Jace said, agreeing with obvious reluctance. "We'll have the sheriff contact the fire department, too, and have them standing by."

Leading the way through the shop to the front door, Rachel asked, "Do you really think there's a bomb?"

"No. But I'd still like to take proper precautions. I don't suppose you happen to know a good electrician."

"I don't know how good he is, but one of the maintenance men over at the courthouse also works for his father's electrical contracting business. If he hears about the trouble, he may drop by and solve our problems."

"You know just about every soul in town, don't you?"

"Probably. Why?"

"Because it gives us a whopping list of suspects."

"Like who?"

"Well, that maintenance man for one. And your old flame, Lance, plus the other guy from church—Adam, wasn't it?"

"No, Alan. Alan Caldwell."

"Okay. And then there's Mrs. McCafferty's nephew, and…"

Reaching the sidewalk she turned and made a face at him. "Do you suspect *everybody?*"

Jace sighed and shrugged. "Afraid so. It goes with the territory. When you've seen the worst of people for a long time, you tend to be on guard in every situation."

"Then you must mistrust me, too," Rachel said. She could tell from the way he'd flinched at her statement that her supposition was correct. "You think *I'm* responsible for all the crazy things that have been happening?"

"I didn't say that."

"No, but you've considered it. Don't bother lying to me. I can see it in your eyes."

Pacing away from him, she fumbled in her purse for her phone. At that moment she wasn't sure whether she was miffed or merely disappointed. Maybe she was both. It was inconceivable that anyone would think she was purposely causing trouble. It made no sense. What was there to gain?

A plausible answer came to mind quickly. If the problems regarding the little card and gift store made the news, it was possible that the notoriety would increase business, if only by bringing in the curious.

Still, it hurt to think that Jace distrusted her, even a tiny bit. He was the one person she had thought she could rely upon and there he stood, implying that she might be the real culprit behind the ongoing harassment.

Her hands were shaking as she flipped open her phone and dialed 9-1-1. If she hadn't felt as if she were suddenly standing alone against her stalker, she might have laughed at the ludicrousness of the idea that she was the cause of all the trouble.

Jace followed the sheriff and several of the firemen back into the building to continue the search and see that the heater was properly disconnected while Rachel waited outside.

He learned that he wasn't the only one who had begun to wonder if she was behind these so-called attacks when Harlan Allgood pulled him aside.

"It seems mighty strange to me," the sheriff said. "I mean, look at what's happened. Nobody was hurt and except for a few dumb notes, there was really no threat."

Jace had to agree. "I know. I thought of that."

"Then what do you reckon is goin' on?" The older man grinned knowingly. "You don't suppose the little lady is sweet on you and just lookin' for a reason the keep you comin' around, do you?"

"I don't know." In Jace's heart there was serious doubt but in his mind the possibility loomed large.

"Well, if I was twenty years younger and not married, I sure wouldn't mind spendin' time with Miss Rachel and that's a fact." He elbowed Jace in the ribs. "She's a pretty one."

"Yes. She is. And she has character, which is why I can't imagine that she's threatening herself. Did you get any fingerprints from the last note?"

"Naw. The preacher's sendin' it off to his citified friends, though. Maybe their lab can find more clues." He guffawed. "If there's any to find."

"What about this time? I didn't see any notes by the thermostat. Did the fire department find anything odd?"

"Not on paper," Harlan said. "C'mon. I'll show you."

Following, Jace continued to scan his surroundings. He was becoming familiar enough with the stock in the shop to guess that little or nothing had been disturbed. Perhaps the heater connections had always been poorly installed or maintained. A building as old as this one would have been retrofitted many times and anything was possible.

"There," Harlan said, pointing. "On that wall."

Jace's heart began to race. There was no paper that they could send to a lab this time. The letters had been scrawled directly on the wall.

It said,

Hot as where I'm going to send you soon, sweetheart. Get ready.

Rachel could tell Jace was upset as soon as he returned to her and she looked into his eyes. "What is it? Was there a bomb?"

"No." He took her arm and guided her away from the small crowd that had gathered in front of the shop and on the courthouse lawn across the street. "But there was another warning."

"What—what did it say?"

"Pretty much the same as before," he told her.

"Where is it? I want to see."

"Later. There's no hurry. Let the others get their pictures and pick up their gear first. The message isn't going anywhere."

"Why not? Isn't Harlan going to give it to Pastor Logan?"

"He can't this time. It's written right on the wall."

"How awful." Studying him so she wouldn't miss any clues to his mood, she asked, "Do you still think I had something to do with all this?" Because he didn't answer immediately, she went on. "Because if you do, I can sort of understand why. I've been thinking about it and I can see that the shop is getting a lot of free publicity. The problem is, it's not the kind of image Eloise and I want for our store."

"I know. And I apologize for doubting you. It just seems incredible that you have no idea who is so mad at you." He smiled slightly. "Harlan thinks you may be doing this to get my attention."

"Oh, really?" Her hands fisted on her hips and she stared at him. "Does he honestly believe I can't get a date without raising a ruckus? He must have been talking to my dad after all."

"I don't think so. I imagine somebody will soon, though. The way the gossip is flying there's no way your father isn't going to find out sooner or later."

"Most likely sooner," Rachel said. "I can hardly wait for the lecture."

"He cares about you."

She sighed loudly. "I know. It's just that he refuses to let me live my own life. He's tried to fix me up with half the men in town."

"Including the electrician?" Jace's eyes narrowed as he looked past her to scan the milling crowd.

"No. Not that I recall."

He had already been standing close to her side. When he moved even nearer, his presence caused her to notice a lack of oxygen in the crisp air.

"This is becoming more than a job to me," Jace said softly. "You do know that, don't you?"

"It shouldn't be," Rachel countered, determined to keep her emotional distance even if she did crave the protectiveness of his physical presence. "I told you. I don't date cops."

"Never?"

"Never ever. Not in a million years." She shook her head theatrically, hoping to soften her statements and still make a point. "Nope. No way. Uh-uh."

"I think I get the idea." To her relief, he was smiling.

"Good. As long as we understand each other."

His eyes began to twinkle with mirth and his grin spread. "I take it that also means I should forget the fact that you kissed me."

"Hey! You started it."

"Yes," he said, chuckling softly, "but you certainly surprised me when you finished it so well."

Blushing, Rachel lowered her gaze and refused to continue to look at him. He was right, of course. She had returned his kiss as instinctively as if they had known each other for ages. He hadn't been the only one surprised. She'd been totally flabbergasted. And ashamed. What must he think of her? That she made a habit of kissing strange men? Probably. Only nothing could be further from the truth.

In all memory, recent and otherwise, she had never been kissed so perfectly, so thoroughly. And she had never, ever, returned the affection with such sureness and ease. Her reaction to Jace's simple kiss had not only knocked her socks off, it had left her wondering how such a wonderful experience had escaped her all these years.

She would never let on that she'd been deeply affected, of course. The man was already so sure of himself that he was practically impossible. More flattery was the last thing he needed, especially coming from her. Next thing she knew, he'd start to believe the sheriff's ridiculous theory that she was causing trouble just to get the new deputy's attention.

There was, however, one thing she wanted him to know, so she decided to speak her mind. "I'm terribly thankful that you were with me today. I hope nothing I've said or done will keep you from continuing to watch over me until this series of attacks stops."

"Of course not. I said I'd look out for you and I will."

She had to blink back tears of relief when she saw the concern on his handsome face. "Thanks. I appreciate it."

His nod was matter-of-fact and polite rather than being too

personal, yet she could tell he was feeling the same sense of extraordinary closeness that she was battling. Surely it was due to the circumstances, she told herself. After all, they had nothing in common.

Except completely opposing opinions of law enforcement personnel. Rachel gritted her teeth as she realized that this ongoing harassment was showing her another side of the picture. There were legitimate needs for police intervention. The problem was, she didn't like feeling out of control or in need of assistance.

She would concentrate on building up her faith, keep her wits about her and get through this, one way or another, she vowed.

When Eloise had led her to the Lord several years back, there had been a change in Rachel. A positive change. It was time she stopped acting as if she were all alone when she knew that Jesus was on her side. She'd pray more and trust more and…

Shivering, she took a step closer to Jace and he slid his arm around her shoulders once again.

Thank You, Father, for putting this man in my life just when I needed him, she prayed silently. If there was ever a reason to give thanks, it was now. And if there was ever a person for whom she was grateful, it was Jace Morgan.

She's clever, but not as clever as she thinks she is, he thought, watching her cozy up to the deputy. *He can't guard her every minute. She'll have to go home sometime and then I'll have her right where I want her.*

He laughed to himself as he imagined future scenarios. He had plenty of ideas about how to make her squirm. And as soon as it stopped being fun to issue threats, he'd act.

There was lots of time. He had already branched out and implemented some new surprises. And even if he didn't get another opportunity to enter the card store in secret, he could simply mail her the special Valentine he'd crafted.

Rachel was going to love his idea of a romantic card. Oh, yes. She was just going to swoon over it.

EIGHT

By the time Rachel and Jace were finally finished at the card shop, it was late afternoon. He had insisted that they needed to go for coffee to pass the time while the professionals did their jobs regarding the crime scene and he'd been surprised by how easily she'd agreed.

There had been only a few brief instances when she had acted afraid, especially when she'd taken a look at the latest communication from her stalker. The rest of the time, if he hadn't known the circumstances, Jace would have assumed she didn't care that much.

"I'm glad I phoned Eloise and filled her in. I was sure she'd decide to close the store for a few days but she says she's game to hang in there if I am. We're going to have to keep our coats on all day though. It's going to stay chilly now that the heater's disconnected."

"Why don't you just call and make an appointment with a repairman to take care of it tomorrow morning?" He smiled. "I know. Don't tell me. You can't arrange anything on a Sunday."

"That's pretty much it," Rachel replied. "But I will call someone tomorrow unless Eloise has already taken care of it. You may think I know a lot of people in this town but I'm a newbie compared to Mrs. McCafferty. Her kin have lived around here for six or seven generations."

"I hadn't thought about the town being that old." He glanced across the square at the brick, three-story, county courthouse. "Guess I should have figured it out by looking at the architecture, huh?"

"And reading the carved text on the monuments on the courthouse lawn," Rachel said. "They mention Civil War battles taking place right here."

"I've heard Harlan call it 'The War Between the States,' instead."

"That's not as politically correct but it is a lot more locally acceptable. Arkansas was part of the South."

"South. Right. That's why I expected to find hot weather down here."

He saw Rachel shiver before she said, "Hot, like the place where my stalker wants to send me?"

"Don't let it get to you." He escorted her to his truck and held the door open while she climbed in. "We'll solve the mystery before long and everything will get back to normal."

Although she smiled and nodded, Jace could tell she wasn't convinced. Neither was he. Whoever had been harassing Rachel was either very clever or amazingly lucky because the sheriff's office hadn't been able to unearth much in the way of clues.

Jace was deep in thought as he pulled away from the curb and they headed for Rachel's house. At least she didn't live on one of those far-out pieces of property that was totally isolated. She had neighbors on both sides of her as well as across the narrow, tree-lined street. That was good. The only thing better would be if he were one of those close neighbors.

"You're awfully quiet," she remarked. "What are you thinking about?"

"You. This area." Leaning slightly forward over the wheel, he peered at the passing homes. "It looks like a good place to live. Is everybody pretty friendly?"

"Very. There are a lot of retired people nearby so I see them often, especially once spring comes and they start gardening."

"And all the houses are occupied?"

"You mean near me, right? Yes. Except for the Duggins place. Floyd died a couple of months ago and his kids haven't decided what to do. I suppose they'll eventually sell the property and split the profits."

"Really?" Jace's mind was spinning. "That gives me an idea. Why don't you get in touch with them and tell them I need a place to live? I wouldn't have to have a lease or anything. Just be sure to stress the fact that I'm Harlan's deputy and can look after it for them. Renting to me has to make more sense than letting it stand vacant and taking the risk that vandals will trash it."

Rachel laughed lightly. "Now you're starting to think like a local. That's a wonderful idea. It's probably even furnished."

"And I'd be closer to you, too, so I could keep an eye on your place at the same time."

It amused him to see the arch of her brows and her lopsided smile so he added, "Well, I could. And any time you needed company, I'd be handy."

"No good," she said, shaking her head and making her hair swing gently. "It might be safer temporarily but it would be terrible for my reputation. Rumors about us are probably already flying. Having you casually come and go, especially after dark, would be disastrous."

"Do you mean to tell me you wouldn't call me in an emergency?"

"I'd call 9-1-1 first."

"And then me."

"Maybe."

There were those rosy cheeks again. Rachel's tendency to blush was endearing. Sandra had never done anything like that, nor had she seemed a bit shy about whether she might be creating a negative impression. Now that he could look back on her behavior and contrast it to Rachel's, he was amazed at how unappealing Sandra's attitude seemed.

The change of perspective caught Jace by surprise. When

had he stopped brooding over his lost love and started seeing her for who and what she really was?

When he'd met Rachel Hollister, he answered without hesitation. It was she who had opened his eyes and given him hope for the future.

His jaw clenched. All he had to do now was make sure Rachel *had* a future. If he didn't put a stop to whomever was threatening her pretty soon, the attacks might escalate until they became deadly.

"I'd ask you in, but…"

"I know. Rumors. Can't have that."

"Right." She held out her hand, expecting him to shake it. Instead, he grasped her fingers in his and simply held them. The intense look in his eyes was so serious it made her pulse speed and her breathing grow ragged.

"Tell you what," Jace said softly, "if I can't come in to stay awhile, how about you leaving the door wide open until we've checked the place over very carefully, just to be on the safe side?"

"You think someone may have been in my house, too?" That notion would have seemed preposterous mere days ago. Now, it made all too much sense to suit her.

"We won't know for sure until we look. Or you could stay outside while I go in and check." He made a motion as if stepping toward the door.

"I'd rather do it myself but you can wait on the porch and watch if you want." Pulling her hand from his grasp she reached for the doorknob and felt his light touch on her shoulder.

"Hold on. Where's your key? Don't you lock your house?"

"I haven't for as long as I've lived here. Nobody does."

"Well, start," Jace grumbled. "I don't believe you country people. Do you trust everybody?"

"Pretty much, yes. We really have very little crime in these parts."

"Yeah, except for the occasional homicidal maniac."

"That's not funny."

"It wasn't meant to be."

Jace was just standing there staring at her, his arms slightly outstretched in a silent plea for understanding. She knew he had a valid point. She also knew that she didn't like the life-style changes she was being forced to make.

"All right. I know I have a house key somewhere. I'll dig it out and start locking my doors. Satisfied?"

"It's a good start," he said. "I'll pick up dead bolts tomorrow."

"You don't have to do that. I can get them."

"When? Last time I looked, your hours were the same as the hardware store's."

"I can run over there on my lunch hour."

"And I can do it as part of my regular patrol. If it's the cost you're worried about, you can repay me later."

"I'll never be able to repay you as well as I should," Rachel said, meaning every word from the bottom of her heart. "I don't know what I'd have done if you hadn't come to my rescue."

"You'd have managed."

"Would I have? I wonder."

"You could have always called your father."

"And listen to him rant and rave and insist that I need a husband to take care of me? No, thanks. Been there, done that. Didn't like it one little bit."

"Is it the idea of marriage that you hate or your dad's choices?"

She huffed. "That's a very good question. I'm not sure. I thought it was both—until recently."

She saw Jace's eyebrows arch. A lump the size of a summer cantaloupe suddenly blocked her throat and stuck there. What in the world was wrong with her? Didn't she have a lick of sense? One tiny kiss and all her decisiveness had flown out the window, along with her common sense—what little she had left of it after being around Jace for the past three days.

Three days? Was that all the time that had passed? Rachel was shocked to realize how briefly they had known each other. There were instances, like now, when it seemed as if they had been acquainted for ages.

And had cared for each other, she added, chagrined. At the least, she was unduly fond of him. Judging by the way he'd been behaving, he might actually share those tender feelings. It was possible. It was also unlikely. A nice fantasy but nothing more.

Was she ready to let a career cop into her dreams, let alone into her life? A short time ago she would have said no. Now, she had to admit she craved his company. The biggest question was, would she feel the same way once her stalker was captured?

Trying to mask a shiver that zigzagged all the way from the nape of her neck to her toes and back again, she insisted he wait on the front porch while she entered the quiet house. Her home. Her sanctuary. The first place in which she had ever felt truly at peace and in control of her life.

Crossing the small living room, she circled the end of the buff-colored leather sofa and proceeded to the sixties-style kitchen, flipping on lights as she went even though the sun had not yet fully set. Everything seemed in order.

"Are you okay?" Jace called through the open door.

"Fine. You can go."

"Not till you check every room. How about the bedrooms?"

"Okay, okay." Rachel shot him a begrudging look as she retraced her steps and headed into the hallway. A sudden chill made her pause.

Jace had apparently been paying close attention to the sound of her footsteps after she passed out of his sight because he shouted, "What's the matter?"

"Nothing. I'm fine. I'll just…" The mayhem which greeted her when she flipped on the bedroom lights took her breath away and made her gasp audibly.

"What? Talk to me, Rachel." When she failed to answer promptly he said, "That does it. I'm coming in."

She was not about to argue. As soon as Jace came up behind her, she turned into his arms and buried her face on his chest so she wouldn't have to look at her bedroom. "Who would do this to me? Why?"

"I don't know," he said flatly. "But you're not staying here tonight. I want you to go to a friend's house. There must be somebody you can stay with. Maybe Logan Malloy and his family. That should be safe enough."

"Look at all my clothes. They're cut to ribbons."

"Yes," Jace said as he guided her back outside. "Maybe this time the person responsible made a mistake and left a clue."

What if they didn't? she wanted to shout. *What if they get away with all this? How much longer can it go on?*

Until they get what they want, Rachel answered as her stomach twisted painfully. *And if the notes are to be believed, they want me dead. Dear God, help me! Please.*

NINE

As Jace had assumed, Logan Malloy was more than happy to help once he had finished officiating at the Sunday evening service. His wife, Becky, had welcomed Rachel like a long lost sister and had immediately ushered her into their home, leaving Jace on the porch with Logan.

"How bad was it?" the pastor asked.

"Bad enough. Very thorough. I left Harlan there with a photographer but I don't know how much they'll be able to tell. All I saw was ripped and cut clothing. Plus, it looked as if whoever did it turned out all the dresser drawers. If there hadn't been those previous instances of threats and break-ins, I might have thought a burglar was looking for something in particular."

"Rachel doesn't think so?"

"No. She insists there was nothing valuable in the house, which leads me back to the vandalism motive."

Raking his fingers through his hair, Logan began to pace. "We haven't gotten anything out of the notes I faxed to Chicago yet, except that my friend thinks they may actually have been written by a child."

Jace frowned. "What? Why?"

"Something about the way the letters were made. He says he'll be able to tell us more once he sees the originals and checks the pressure of the crayons on the paper. He insists that an adult would write differently, even if he were trying to emulate childish efforts."

"How odd. And interesting." Jace paused, then added, "Hey. Wait a minute. If this guy is using a real kid to print the notes, what about the writing on the wall? Surely, he wouldn't take a child into the store with him. It would pose an unnecessary risk."

"I agree. The first thing I want to do is get copies of those pictures of the wall that were taken this afternoon. I think you and I should head over to Rachel's place, too, and help Harlan."

Jace smiled. "Help him? Don't you mean see that he doesn't mess up too badly?"

"Something like that." The pastor chuckled and reached for the doorknob. "Just let me tell Becky where we're going."

"Hold it. Is it safe for us to leave the women alone?"

That question brought more soft laughter. "My wife is a true country girl," Logan said. "She's not afraid of guns and knows how to properly handle them if need be. They'll be as safe as if you and I were standing guard."

"If you say so. I haven't been doing so well in that regard. It seems like the more I try to protect Rachel, the worse the situation gets."

"Only because this guy has been one step ahead of us. He can't keep it up without stumbling. One of us will nail him."

"As long as it happens before he carries out the threats he's been making," Jace said soberly. "I'm really worried about Rachel."

"A lot of folks are praying for her." He clapped Jace on the shoulder as he passed. "Wait for me. I'll be right back as soon as I talk to Becky."

I think it's going to take more than prayer, Jace told himself as the pastor went inside. *I think it's going to take every trick I know, and more. I just hope that's enough.* He grimaced. *It had better be.*

The hours she spent away from Jace were the longest in Rachel's memory. Drinking tea and nibbling cookies with

Becky Malloy would have been a lot more pleasant if they had not discussed the threats in such depth. By the time the men returned to the house, Rachel was so emotionally and physically worn out she could barely keep her eyes open.

One look at the concern on Jace's face, however, awakened her fully. She jumped to her feet and went to meet him before he and Logan had come halfway across the living room. "What is it? What did you two find out?"

"Not a whole lot," Logan said. He bent and kissed his wife as Jace slipped an arm lightly around Rachel's shoulders.

Jace nodded. "He's right. Harlan is bagging your clothes, what was left of them, to send to the lab in Little Rock, but it didn't look promising to either of us."

"We're right back where we started?"

"Not entirely," Jace said. "At least there was no threatening note found this time. Come and sit down. Pastor Logan has an idea."

Rachel let herself be guided to the sofa. Jace sat next to her while Becky took a matching chair and Logan paced in a confined oval in front of them.

"It's time we set a trap," Logan said. "Jace and I have talked it over and…"

Becky was quick to object. "Uh-uh. No way. This is not like the trouble I had with my family a few years back. This person is bent on either scaring poor Rachel to death or doing actual harm. There's no way you two can dangle her out there like spinner bait in a bass tournament. I won't allow it."

"Yes, Mama," Logan teased. He turned to Rachel with a grin. "She's been like this ever since our Timmy was born. As protective as a mother tiger."

"I can use that kind of protection right now," Rachel said.

Jace reached for her hand and she not only allowed him to grasp it, she wove her fingers between his.

"Something Becky just said gave me another thought," Jace said. "I'm sorry to suggest this, Rachel, but is it possible that your own father is trying to scare you into listening to his advice and doing things his way?"

Her first reaction was to take offense. In the space of a heartbeat, however, she realized that it just might be possible. She'd known her stubborn, self-righteous father to go to great lengths to get his way with her mother, so what was to say he wouldn't lie to keep his grown daughter in line? Then, she remembered her destroyed wardrobe and made up her mind.

"I started to say I don't know. But that was when I was only considering the earlier threats and silly notes. Dad is hard-headed but he'd never be as mean as whoever it was who ruined my clothes."

"I agree," Logan said. "I've known George Hollister since I've lived in Serenity. He may be opinionated to a fault but he's not vindictive. No. It's somebody else. Somebody who thinks Rachel has done something bad to them."

She shivered. "But who? I wouldn't hurt a fly. Not on purpose."

"We know that," Jace said. "I've discussed it with Pastor Logan and we've decided to take turns keeping an eye on you. If you can get me into that house near yours it will simplify matters, but even if you can't, we'll manage."

"I hate to put you to all that trouble. Maybe Becky could stay with me, instead."

It did nothing to calm her fears when both Logan and Jace adamantly rejected that idea. Clearly, neither of them wanted to jeopardize Becky's safety, which left Rachel feeling exactly like the bait the other woman had mentioned.

No matter which man was keeping watch, her enemy might outwit him and get into her house or shop anyway. If she came face-to-face with someone so evil, so bent on harming her, would she recognize him for what he was?

She certainly hoped so, because the way things were going, she was pretty sure it wouldn't be long before she and her stalker met. Her only true defense was her faith. And the fresh can of Mace in her purse, a secret gift from the pastor's wife.

* * *

It was another week before Rachel could get Jace to commit to letting her return to her normal routine. He had been visiting the shop so regularly that Eloise had begun referring to him as Rachel's shadow.

"I don't want you going back to your house until Logan and I are all set up," Jace said in answer to Rachel's most recent query.

"Phooey. I need to go home. My potted plants must be dying from lack of water by now. Besides, I'm sick of imposing on the Malloys."

"One more day. Just one more. I've got my stuff moved into the Duggins place and Logan is almost through setting up the cameras. We'd be done already if we weren't taking pains to make sure we aren't seen."

"In my neighborhood there's little chance of getting away with anything," Rachel countered. "But have it your way." She began to scowl. "You aren't going to be watching me inside, too, are you?"

"Only in the living room and kitchen. Don't worry. Most of the surveillance will be concentrated on the outer perimeter of the property."

"Meaning, if he gets by that, I'm on my own."

"Not at all." He'd been waiting for the right moment to go over the entire plan and couldn't think of a better opportunity than this. "We'll set up a code system you can use to let us know if there's a problem."

"How about a nice, loud scream? I can do that."

Jace had to laugh. "I was thinking more of a word or two that would fit into normal conversation. If there's no immediate threat, we'd rather capture the guy red-handed, so to speak."

"Blood is red," she said with a grimace. "Just make sure it isn't mine, okay?"

He stepped closer and held out his arms, hoping she would accept the comfort of an innocent embrace. Not that it would be so innocent on his part, he admitted ruefully. The more time he spent with Rachel, the more emotionally involved he became, like it or not. And he wasn't sure if he did like it. After all, she had made her position regarding police officers quite clear. Unless something happened to erase all the damage done by her father's attitude of superiority, there was little chance she'd ever consider getting serious about marrying a cop.

That surprising thought brought him up short. Marry? Him? No way. He was just feeling connected due to his professional concern for a crime victim, that was all.

And then Rachel stepped into his embrace, wiping away every misgiving, every doubt. As Jace closed his arms around her and she slipped hers around his waist, she laid her head on his shoulder.

The closeness that had developed between them was not simple, nor was it harmless, he realized. Their relationship had deepened in a few short days until it was much more than that of victim and protector. He cared about this young woman far too much to be able to reason his feelings away or laugh them off.

For Jace, that was nearly as scary as it would have been for him to have become the focus of the stalker's ire. He wished he could somehow step between Rachel and her nemesis and relieve her of that burden once and for all.

Sighing, he hugged her and prayed silently for the opportunity to do just that.

"My car is safely locked in the garage and I have the only remote control so I'll be able to drive to and from work from now on," Rachel told Jace.

"Good. Pastor Logan and I don't want you to walk anymore, especially not until daylight savings time starts."

"I know, I know. And I won't after today." Rachel prepared to close the shop. "As soon as I get home, I'll phone you on your cell. You and Logan will be able to see everything. Right?"

"Right."

"It'll be okay." She reached up and patted his cheek. "You're the guys with the plan. Don't you trust it?"

"Sure we do. I just…"

"You worry too much. We haven't had a single bad thing happen around here in over a week. Not even accidentally. Maybe whoever was mad at me gave up after he trashed my clothes." She didn't believe that for a second. Unfortunately, she could tell from Jace's expression that he didn't, either.

"I promise I'll take all the precautions we discussed," Rachel said. "I have my Mace handy, too. Nobody is going to hurt me."

"Just see that you don't panic and use it on the wrong guys," Jace told her. "I had the experience of being sprayed with it in training and it wasn't fun."

"I'm sure it wasn't. Becky tells me it will stop a grown man in his tracks."

"A normal man, yes. Anybody who's on drugs or is otherwise deranged may be another story."

"Point taken," Rachel said, smiling. "Look, are you going to get out of the way and let me finally go home or not?"

To her chagrin he stepped aside without insisting on a parting hug. Such innocent expressions of affection were an integral part of Southern custom and Rachel hadn't thought much of it until Jace had started emulating the locals. His hugs were definitely not as platonic as most. The mere thought of them made her blush.

She scooped up her purse and keys and headed for the door. "The back is locked, including the new dead bolt. Come on. Time to go."

Although she knew she sounded unconcerned, it was all an act. Inside, she was trembling so badly her stomach was upset and she had a tension headache that ran all the way from her shoulders to her throbbing temples.

The few new clothes she'd bought to add to those Becky had loaned her had already been delivered to her house and were, hopefully, waiting. There had been little salvageable among her damaged personal belongings, making the incident even more traumatic.

Leaving Jace to follow at a discrete distance, she started up Main and turned down Third Street, walking boldly with her head held high, knowing that each step was bringing her that much closer to finding out who was so bent on destroying her peace of mind.

"If that's all they end up doing, then praise the Lord," Rachel murmured, trying to reason away some of her fear.

It was no use. The nearer she got to her house, the more she trembled. Her throat felt as dry as the native creeks in August. Her hands shook like leaves in a gale.

She paused in the street and stared at the neat, brick-fronted home that she had always viewed as her one sanctuary. Now, it loomed like a forbidding cave filled with unnamed monsters. The windows were dark as if hiding an unspeakable terror that was lying in wait. For her.

TEN

Jace took the first official watch. And the second. He figured it was best to give himself something constructive to do rather than simply pace the floor. Besides, he was the one actually living in the house they were using as a base of operations so that made more sense than having Logan come over and do it.

Jace had been on plenty of stakeouts before. Basically, they consisted of hours of boredom interspersed with a few seconds of sheer bedlam. So far, all he had to show for his efforts in respect to Rachel was a throbbing headache and stiff shoulder muscles.

He rubbed his neck. Walked back and forth. Grabbed a sandwich even though he wasn't hungry and ate it sitting next to the monitors.

The cameras that were trained on Rachel's place were set to record when there was movement within range. Otherwise, they merely showed a live feed and let him listen to her humming as she spruced up her house after being gone so long.

If he hadn't been looking right at the screen when she said "I've missed you. Did you miss me, too?" he might have thought she had company. Instead, she was bending over a large, fernlike plant and tipping up a watering can.

"The woman talks to her houseplants," he murmured, disgusted by the way his heart had leaped when he'd heard her voice.

He took out his cell phone and did what he'd been wanting to do for the past hour or more. Rachel's home number was on speed dial, as was that of her shop.

She answered on the first ring. "Hello?"

"It's just me. You scared me silly."

"Why?" Jace saw her stare directly at the hidden camera. Her eyes were wide and she was definitely apprehensive. "Is somebody sneaking up on me?"

"No, no. You were talking to your fern, I guess, and I thought for a wild second that it was a person."

"Nope." Relaxing, she grinned. "Very few people sit around in clay pots and have green fronds for hair. That's how you can tell the difference." She giggled. "It always works for me."

"Thanks for the tip." Jace knew he shouldn't have called her but something inside him had insisted. "Sorry I bothered you."

"It's no bother," she said, once again smiling at the camera.

"You might want to stop talking to that lens as if it was me," he cautioned. "If somebody is watching, you might scare him off."

"Scaring him off sounds good to me." Rachel sobered and shrugged. "I get the point, though. You want me to seem vulnerable."

"It's an illusion. You're perfectly safe. I can be there in seconds if you give the word."

"Oh, sure, but how am I going to find a way to work *Valentine* into my conversation to tip you off?"

"You run a card shop. It shouldn't be that difficult."

"Right. Okay. I just want this all to be over."

"Believe me," Jace said, "so do I."

When there was a loud thud at her door, Rachel's first instinct was to hurry to see what had happened. Then, she had second thoughts. Before pulling aside the blinds and peering out the front window, she flipped on the porch light and grabbed her phone to have it in hand in case she needed it.

She squinted. Nothing was moving. No one was visible. The moon was full and streetlights also illuminated the area all the way to the street. Nothing seemed amiss.

"Doors do not knock by themselves," she said aloud, assuming Jace or Logan could hear her. "What should I do? I don't see a soul outside. Do you?"

Pausing with her cell in her hand, she waited for it to ring with her answer. Nothing happened.

All right, Rachel reasoned, she had two options. She could either leave the door locked or open it and see for herself what was going on. In the movies, the heroine always made the most foolish choices and got herself into all kinds of trouble. She was smarter than that. She knew she could leave the locks engaged and call Jace or Pastor Logan to come over and see if there was anything wrong on her porch.

"Except that that seems cowardly," she told herself. "And stupid. If they show themselves and someone sees them do it, all their careful plans to catch my stalker will be for nothing."

She put down the phone and picked up the tiny can of Mace. One peek. That was all she needed. If she cracked open the door and didn't see anything on her porch, she'd slam it again, lock it up tight and no one would be the wiser.

With trembling hands she twisted the dead bolt till she heard it click. Turning the knob slowly, cautiously, she held the Mace in front of her like a shield and eased open the door. The porch was empty.

Letting out a noisy sigh she was about to lock up again when she looked down and spotted something white lying on the welcome mat. It was a plain envelope.

She crouched. One arm snaked out just far enough to grab the envelope and pull it inside before she slammed the door hard and leaned against it.

Her pulse was pounding. Her breathing was shallow. Her

fingers trembled. If it had not been for the previous threatening notes she wouldn't have been concerned, but she was afraid that this was another one. If it was, it had to have been recently placed there. Why hadn't Jace seen someone lurking? Why hadn't he phoned? And who in the world could have gotten past the defenses he and Logan had installed without being spotted?

She slipped her index finger under the flap and tore the envelope open. Its contents were not another cryptic note, as she had feared. Instead, it was a morbid Valentine. There was a picture of a heart, all right, but it was mounted on a black background and there was a drawing of a dagger piercing it.

Rachel swayed, suddenly dizzy, as she opened the card. The printing inside swam before her eyes. It was more of the same childish scrawl and this time it said,

It's almost time to celebrate, darling.
Happy Valentine's Day.

Her phone jangled. She dropped the card as she answered, assuming the caller was Jace.

"It's—it's a Valentine," she said in a near whisper.

Rather than the encouragement she had expected, someone gave a hoarse laugh and said, "I know. I'm glad you like it, sweetheart."

Rachel dropped the phone with a shriek, took a deep breath, looked up at the camera and announced loudly, "It's a *Valentine!*"

Jace vaulted off the back porch of the Duggins house and raced across the rear yards of the two other properties that lay between him and Rachel. His sidearm was secure in its holster. One fist was clenched around a heavy flashlight.

He tried to phone her as he ran and wasn't able to get through so he stuck the phone in his pocket to free his gun hand. In seconds he was rounding the front corner of her house and taking the porch steps two at a time.

She threw open the door and welcomed him with open arms. Unshed tears lurked behind the fear he saw immediately. Pushing her aside and stepping in front to act as a human shield, he drew his pistol and crouched, ready to do battle.

"Where is he?" Jace demanded.

"I don't know."

Keeping his concentration focused on their surroundings, he insisted on a clearer reply. "What do you mean, you don't know? Did you see him or not?"

"No."

"Then why did you use the code word? I told you…"

"I know what you told me," Rachel answered, sounding almost as miffed as she did frightened. She thrust her hand forward and displayed a black-rimmed card. "This was just delivered. Didn't you see who did it?"

"No. The cameras didn't pick up a thing." Although he started to relax he didn't holster the gun because he was far from satisfied that there was no imminent danger. "Where did you find that?"

"On the porch."

That was shocking enough to command Jace's full attention. "You *what?* Haven't you listened to a thing Logan and I have told you? What part of *keep the doors locked* don't you understand?"

"I heard something. And I asked you if you saw anything but you didn't answer."

"What are you talking about?" Watching her face and seeing how truly confused and panicky she was, he realized he'd been shouting at her. "Okay. Start from the beginning. What happened, exactly?"

"I—I heard a noise on the porch."

"A knock?"

"Kind of. Now that I think about it, it was more of a thud."

"Then what?"

"I don't remember exactly. I think I talked to the camera again and was expecting you to phone me."

"I tried. Your line was busy." He saw her glance at the place on the rug where her phone lay.

"I did get a call, only it wasn't you. It was him. I—I guess I dropped the phone. The rest you know."

"All right." Jace slipped one arm around Rachel's shoulders, hoping she wouldn't notice that he was trembling. Every muscle in his body was knotted, every nerve fiber on alert. Even when he'd been caught in the line of fire in the past, he had not reacted so strongly. Not even when he'd been shot.

Whether Rachel realized it or not, the stalker was escalating his approach. He'd not only left the morbid-looking Valentine, he'd actually spoken to her on the phone. That was not a good sign. Not good at all.

Worse, he had somehow placed the card on her porch without being photographed by the surveillance equipment. That, alone, raised the hackles on Jace's neck.

"Okay," he said, trying to sound calm and in control. "You stay right here, inside, while I take a look at the porch. If there's no malfunction of the cameras, they should pick me up and record my actions."

She was clinging to him. "Why do you have to go out there? He's obviously gone."

"Mainly to test the cameras," Jace explained. "And I want to see if I can figure out how he managed to knock without setting foot on the porch."

"That's impossible."

"Nothing is impossible. It's just a matter of figuring it out so he doesn't get away with the same thing again."

Although Rachel shuddered, she did release her hold. "Okay. Go do it. But you're coming back inside as soon as you're done."

"What about the neighbors?"

To his relief she gave him a lopsided smile and said, "Let the neighbors get their own cop."

Jace nodded. "Right. I'm all yours, at least till we have a chance to alert Logan and tell him what's happened. I'm going to want him to check the entire system and since he'll be watching our every move, he can testify that you and I were behaving ourselves. That should quiet the rumormongers."

He placed a conciliatory kiss on her forehead as he stepped away. "I'll be right back. And then we'll see if we can trace that call."

"Don't be long. And don't go far. Promise?"

A few tears slid down her cheeks as he watched, touching his heart in a way that was so tender it almost undid him. "I promise," he said softly. "I'm just going to the porch steps."

"What if he's still out there?"

"I doubt he will be," Jace told her. "But even if he is, I can handle myself. I'm a pro, remember?"

"You've never made a mistake?"

"Only once when it counted," he replied, thinking of the night he and his partner were ambushed. "And I won't do that again."

Rather than answer the personal questions he assumed would ensue, he turned off the porch light and began to open the front door. Just then a startling thought popped into his head. "Hold it. I came in this way. It was unlocked."

"Only because I had just picked up the Valentine."

"Lock it after me. Now."

Her eyebrows arched and she dashed away the sparse tears that had wet her cheeks. "No way. I'm going to stand right here and keep an eye on you, whether you like it or not. You're not getting out of my sight."

Jace opened his mouth to argue, then decided against wasting his breath. Judging by her firm expression, Rachel was not going to listen to reason. And, in a way, he didn't blame her. He was used to this kind of thing and he, too, was on edge, so she must be close to panic. If keeping him in sight would help her cope, he wasn't going to deny her that comfort.

"Okay, but turn off the inside lights so you're not silhouetted in the doorway. The darker it is, the better."

"Gotcha."

Slowly stepping onto the porch, he crouched, prepared for an attack. None came. His eyes adjusted to the dimness. The neighborhood was so quiet it was spooky. Half the houses were dark and the rest showed light only in one or two windows, probably because the occupants were watching television.

Jace straightened. Took one step, then another. He looked down. A rough-edged rock the size of a softball lay near the edge of the wooden decking. He flicked on his flashlight and directed it at the outside of the half-open door.

"What are you doing?" Rachel asked. "I thought you wanted me to be in the dark."

"I did. I do. But come around and look at that mark on the porch. I think I know what happened."

"You do? What?"

"I think he managed to place the envelope on your porch between the time you got home and I got to the surveillance equipment and turned it on. Then, all he had to do was wait for dark and throw a rock at your door to get you to open it."

Jace saw her shiver and wrap her arms around herself. "You know what that means?"

"Yes," he said soberly. "It means he's a lot smarter than we've given him credit for. And he was very, very close to both of us."

ELEVEN

Rachel wasn't sure she would ever feel safe again, no matter where she was or who was looking out for her. The past week was a blur, partly because she hadn't slept well and partly because every time she dozed off her dreams were filled with a sense of impending doom.

Not only that, her father had confronted Pastor Logan and the sheriff, found out what was going on, and had insisted that he be included in the rotating surveillance team. Although he would not have been her first choice to keep watch, she had to admit that his presence was allowing the other men to get some much needed rest.

While Pastor Logan and her father took turns keeping watch in the Duggins house, Jace slept on Rachel's sofa, well chaperoned by the others via the camera system. At this point, she was far less worried about her reputation than she was about surviving. And she trusted Jace implicitly. The only problem might be unfounded gossip, and, the way she saw it, that was the least of her worries.

The sheriff's office had failed to trace the threatening call, and the labs in both Arkansas and Illinois had provided no additional clues. However, since the arrival of the black-edged Valentine, Rachel's life had been fairly uneventful. She'd spent quiet days with Eloise in the card store, had eaten most of her meals out, and had welcomed Jace to his place on her sofa each evening.

She was getting pretty comfortable about his continued presence, she noticed, not at all sure whether or not that was a good thing. Eloise, of course, was privy to all the details, including the temporary arrangements for live-in protection, and had vowed to keep Rachel's secret for as long as was necessary.

"I think you should do like Becky Malloy and learn to shoot," Eloise remarked as soon as she and Rachel had finished with their most recent customer and were alone in the shop.

"I'd probably get nervous and shoot myself in the foot," Rachel said, smiling. "Besides, how often would I need to defend myself?"

"I don't know. Once is too often if you ask me. If this situation wasn't serious, I doubt that Harlan would be patrolling your street so often or that that nice young deputy would be sleeping on your couch."

"Hush. You'll start gossip."

"No need to worry. There's plenty going around already. I'll sure be glad when I can spill the beans and tell everybody that Pastor Malloy and your dad are watching over you while that man is sleeping in your house. Otherwise, you'll never live it down."

"I know. I wish there were some other way to handle the situation, but Jace is afraid to leave me alone."

"Well, the whole plan strikes me as foolish," Eloise said. "There must be some other way to catch whoever is harassing you." As she spoke, she was straightening the card racks.

Rachel stepped up and helped her. "I thought it was a good idea at first. But since they've made no progress, I wonder."

"It is a shame how times have changed since I was a girl," Eloise said. "I remember when Delbert was courting me." She smiled wistfully. "He was so shy it was cute. We used to sit on the porch swing at my parents' farmhouse and hold hands and talk for hours, even in the summer when the skeeters were biting something awful."

"I wish…"

The older woman arched a gray eyebrow. "You wish what? That you could find a man like him? Well, there was only one like my Delbert, but that Jace Morgan fella seems pretty sweet on you."

"He's just doing his job," Rachel insisted.

"Oh, yeah? Since when do cops volunteer to sleep on people's couches? You can't fool me, dear. You and he are an item, as they say in the supermarket tabloids."

"We're not. Not really." Rachel felt her cheeks warming. "At least not on his part. He wouldn't be anywhere near me unless he felt he had to be."

"Who says? Him?"

"Well, no, but…"

Before she could express the thought completely, Eloise gasped. She was making a sour face when she looked at Rachel. "Mercy me, girl. I know some of my choices are a bit old-fashioned, but don't you think that's a bit much for the folks in Serenity?"

"What is?"

Eloise pointed. "That card. I've heard about those kids who mope around, dress all in black and even paint their fingernails that color. They call themselves Goths or something. Surely you don't mean to encourage them." She reached toward the black-edged card she'd found tucked behind a classic Valentine.

"Don't touch that!" Rachel shouted. "Get away from it."

"Why? Is there something wrong?"

"Yes." Rachel knew she was shaking as she grabbed a phone and dialed 9-1-1. "This is Rachel Hollister at Serenity Cards and Gifts," she said as soon as the dispatcher answered. "Send somebody over right away. I've had another contact."

"I don't know how it got there," Rachel told Jace and the sheriff. Harlan merely huffed, tugged at the gun belt below his paunch and walked out of the store.

Jace lingered. He'd already bagged the suspect card in plastic but he hated to just leave without making sure Rachel was going to be okay.

"I get off duty in a few hours," he said. "Want to meet me for supper? We can always grab another pizza at Hickory Station."

"I'd really rather just go home and crash," she said. "This whole mess has worn me out."

He massaged the back of his neck, remembering the kinks he always got in it while sleeping on her sofa. "Yeah. Me, too. How about letting me get takeout, then? We can eat it under Logan's or your father's watchful eye."

"They must be exhausted, too. How much longer does this have to go on?"

"Until we catch the guy," Jace said flatly. "I'm sorry it's taking so long. I was beginning to think he'd given up until you found this card."

"So was I." She shuddered visibly and glanced at the neat racks of colorful greeting cards. "I can't understand how anyone could have placed it without us noticing."

"It could have been *anybody,*" Eloise piped up. "What is this old world coming to?"

"There are good and bad people everywhere, even here," Jace said. "Are you two sure you checked all the slots? There're no other cards like this?"

"Absolutely," Rachel said. "We even went through the extra stock in the drawers. There was just the one."

"Okay. I'll see you around five-thirty, quarter to six." He forced a smile in the hopes it would calm Rachel's jitters. "Pepperoni and mushroom with extra cheese, right?"

"That sounds fine," she said.

Eloise laughed. "Gotta love a fella who remembers just what a lady likes," she said with a wink. "I don't know about Rachel, here, but you've convinced me you're a real prince, young man."

"Thank you, ma'am. I do aim to please." He touched the

brim of his cap in parting and headed for the door, hoping he didn't look as worried as he really was.

Harlan might not think this was a serious event, but Jace did. The person who had placed that card had been within reach of Rachel, meaning she wasn't safe even in public. There was little more he could do, yet his mind—and his heart—kept insisting that he act.

As he climbed into the patrol car and dropped the bagged card onto the seat beside him, he sighed deeply. He had made the worst mistake any officer could make—he had gotten emotionally involved with a victim and was therefore less able to remain objective, especially in regard to her ongoing safety.

What he wanted to do was take Rachel in his arms and hold her tight against any whisper of danger, now or in the future. And because that was physically impossible, he was so distracted that his brain was practically useless. Yes, he had implemented a clever plan. And, yes, they were continuing to keep watch, both in person when Rachel was home and by leaving the videotape running even when she was gone. Still, there had to be something else he could do, something he was overlooking.

He shook his head in disgust. As far as he knew, he and the others had taken all necessary steps. So why had they failed to nab the suspect? And how much longer were Pastor Logan and George Hollister going to be able to stand watch? Logan would probably have to back off soon in order to resume his normal pastoral duties, and then the whole task would fall to George.

If Harlan had been scheduled to take a shift it would have helped, but Jace and Rachel both preferred having Logan and her father do it, primarily because their presence lent a sense of tacit approval to the touchy situation. As long as those men were watching, they knew there would be far less criticism of their unusual sleeping arrangements once they could make the whole story public.

"And I do care about preserving Rachel's good reputation," Jace told himself. "She's a very special person."

That's the understatement of the century, he added silently, dismayed. In the space of mere weeks she had become the most important woman in his life. If things worked out, he was hoping she would consider becoming a permanent part of the rest of his days.

He huffed. *No sweat.* All he had to do was make sure she survived her stalker, then change her mind about cops after a lifetime of her father's negative influence.

Maybe tonight, as they shared their evening meal, he'd raise the subject of a possible romantic relationship, especially if George wasn't the one on duty. That way, Jace could watch Rachel's expression and judge whether or not she accepted his suggestion.

He didn't know which was going to be harder to deal with in the long run: threats of danger or Rachel's off-putting attitude. He suspected it might be a toss-up.

The rest of the day seemed to drag by. Rachel checked her watch repeatedly, then locked the shop door several minutes early. Eloise had already gone home, complaining about sore feet and worsening arthritis due to an impending storm front, and Rachel didn't much like being left in the quiet store alone.

All afternoon she had racked her brain, trying to recall each customer who had dropped by that day. It was no use. They all ran together in her memory until she was unable to tell one from another. Besides, she reasoned, there was an outside chance that the distressing card had been placed in that rack a long time prior to its discovery. Just because no one had noticed it did not mean that its presence was new.

That thought gave her the shivers. She grabbed her keys, locked up and hurried to her car. The moment she was safely behind the wheel she locked those doors, too.

It was a few minutes after five-thirty and there was no sign of Jace or his familiar patrol car. He had probably meant he'd pick up the pizza and they'd meet at her house rather than here, she reasoned.

Yearning to be home and feel safe again, she started the compact car and pulled into the street. Once she and Jace were together again she'd be able to unwind, she told herself. At least she wouldn't be fearful.

As far as really relaxing was concerned, however, she wasn't all that calm in his presence. It was comforting to be with him. It was also exhilarating. And pleasant beyond reason. She looked forward to their time together as if he were her reason for living, the sunshine in her otherwise drab life.

Admitting that, even to herself, was scary. She was no fool. She knew exactly what was going on. She had stupidly fallen for a cop, of all people, and she had no earthly idea what to do about it.

Earthly idea, no, she affirmed. But God was in charge of her life so He was the one to ask. She wanted to pray. Sort of. Except she was afraid she might not like the divine answer she received. If God had not placed Jace Morgan in her life so that he would become a lasting part of it, perhaps he was simply the method the Good Lord was using to rid her of her prejudice against officers like her father.

That notion stuck in her mind and refused to be banished. Surely, after all she'd been through, she was not going to lose Jace. That wouldn't be fair.

"Yeah, assuming there's anything to lose," she muttered as she pulled into her driveway and pushed the button on the garage door opener.

The partitioned door rolled up, section by section, then stopped at the top of its arc.

Rachel slowly drove into the garage and triggered the control again to drop and secure the door behind her.

Lost in her musings, she sighed and remained in the car until the garage was safely closed. When all this was over, she certainly hoped Jace would continue to visit, to want to keep seeing her, because if not, she was going to be terribly lonely. The solitude she had enjoyed in the past no longer appealed. Now, all she wanted was to be with him, to talk to him, to see his smile and lose herself in the wonders of his deep blue gaze.

Getting out of the car, she left her headlights on to illuminate the small garage. What was wrong with the motion sensor on the overhead light? It was supposed to come on automatically, whenever anyone or anything passed.

Looking up, Rachel squinted. The bulb was gone from the fixture! How could that have happened? And when? She'd left everything locked up tight when she'd gone to work and the only other way in was via the touch pad mounted outside. As far as she knew, she and Jace were the only ones privy to that secret number sequence.

Concerned and a bit confused, she reached for the knob on the door leading to her kitchen and tried to turn it. It wouldn't budge. Locked? How could it be locked? That door was *never* locked. She didn't have the key for it with her because she saw no need to carry it. After all, the garage door was secure.

The hair on the back of her neck prickled a primitive warning. Had something on the opposite side of the car just made a scuffing noise? Rachel froze. She fisted her key ring in one hand while she rummaged in her purse for the can of Mace.

Could she hear breathing? Was it hers? She held her breath and listened to her own pulse thudding in her ears. She was trapped in that tiny garage, unless…

Diving for the car, she jammed her thumb against the remote control button on the visor, fully expecting the heavy garage door to start to lift.

Nothing happened. She slammed the car door behind her and locked it with her left hand while continuing to try to work the remote. It had functioned fine a few seconds ago. Why was it not working now?

The glare from her compact car's headlights nearly blinded her as she stared out the windshield. Something moved to her right. A shadow shifted. A man-size one. And it was coming closer.

TWELVE

Jace set the box with the hot pizza next to him on the seat of his patrol car, backed out of the Hickory Station parking lot and headed straight for the card shop. He was glad he'd told Rachel to wait for him because he didn't want her going home alone.

Thinking back over their conversation as he drove, he realized that he had not specified where she was to meet him. Surely she'd understood what he'd meant. She knew better than to go home unescorted, even though they had changed all her locks and reprogrammed her garage door opener.

As he pulled even with the card store, however, he realized that her car was already gone. His pulse began to pound and his heart leaped. "What was she thinking?"

That I was going to meet her at the house, he answered only in his mind. How typical. She'd wanted to go home so she had conveniently assumed that that was what they'd agreed upon.

Whipping the wheel and making a U-turn, he was thankful that there was no cross traffic. It was only a short distance to Rachel's and she couldn't have been gone long. He'd probably be able to overtake her in a couple of minutes at the most.

His hands fisted on the steering wheel. A few minutes was all it would take for someone to end her life.

Jace tasted bile. His jaw clenched. Every sense was heightened as he pressed hard on the accelerator. The tires of the patrol car squealed around the corner onto Third Street.

Squinting, he tried to see far enough ahead to tell if Rachel was parked in her driveway.

He didn't see her car. He didn't see any cars. So where was she? And why had she refused to wait for him? Had she been abducted? Was he too late?

Deep in his mind he could visualize her in trouble. The image wasn't a logical one. But it was so clear, so intense, he felt as if he were viewing reality.

"Dear God," he prayed. "Tell me what to do. Where is she?"

Rachel was terrified. Trapped. Helpless. The car doors were locked and she was temporarily safe inside, but what if her stalker smashed the windows? What then? If he'd spent any amount of time lurking in the garage he had to have discovered that there were hand tools available. A hammer would shatter her side windows and then all he'd have to do is reach in and grab her.

She must not allow that to happen. But what other options did she have?

A shadow clad all in black crossed in front of the right headlight and stopped perpendicular to the hood of the car. It bent over. Rachel gasped. Was he trying to open the hood? It sure looked like it. And if he was successful, he'd be able to disable the car and stop her from starting it.

Of course! Her would-be assailant's actions had answered her question. With the engine running she'd at least be maneuverable, even if she wasn't able to back out with the door closed.

She turned the key. The car started. The shadowy figure raised both arms and jumped aside.

Rachel wanted to cheer. She'd surprised him, all right. Now what? If he got in front of her again she could run into him, pin him between her bumper and the end wall, but that didn't solve the problem of her current vulnerability.

Did she dare try to back her car through the closed door? Was there enough room to get a little momentum going and actually break out? And if she tried and failed, would it just make matters worse?

That notion almost made her laugh hysterically. "Worse? How could this get any worse?"

In an instant she knew. The window on the passenger side shattered into a million tiny pieces and many of them rained onto the seat beside her. A black-clad arm reached through, grasping blindly.

That was all the incentive Rachel needed. Flooring the accelerator, she backed straight into the partitioned door.

To her horror, it splintered but held.

The arm came at her again.

She screamed. Ducked. Roared forward till her front bumper smacked the wall, then once again jammed the car into Reverse.

The tires spun and whistled against the cement floor. This time, the door gave and she rocketed out onto the driveway.

Jace saw the base panels of the door splinter and fall away. He skidded the patrol car to a stop across the drive to block it and was nearly hit broadside by the car that was racing toward him.

He bailed out the driver's door, drew his gun and crouched, ready for anything. When Rachel practically fell out of her car he ran to her side.

"What happened?"

She pointed. "He's there. In the garage. He…"

Jace didn't wait for her full explanation. Pushing her down, he ordered, "Stay here," and was gone in a flash. The headlights of her car illuminated the hole she'd smashed in the door and he caught a glimpse of movement.

"Freeze! Police," he shouted.

The figure ducked back into the shadows. "I knew you wouldn't make this easy," he grumbled. "That suits me just fine."

Before proceeding, he turned back to check on Rachel. She was crouched just where he'd left her. "Go to my car and use the radio to call for backup," Jace shouted. "And lock yourself in."

As soon as she waved and started to obey he returned his concentration to the damaged garage. Rachel had surprised him with her resourcefulness and willingness to destroy property in order to save herself. She was one of a kind, all right. The perfect woman for him.

But before he told her so, he had a job to do. One he was going to thoroughly enjoy.

Raising up and keeping his gun trained on the hole, he started to inch forward.

Rachel yanked open the passenger side door of the patrol car and threw herself inside, realizing belatedly that she was sitting on a now collapsed pizza box.

She wasn't all that familiar with a police radio but since this was such a small department she figured it would be tuned to the right frequency and therefore pretty easy to use.

She grabbed the microphone, pressed the side to trigger it, and shouted, "Harlan, Jace needs help. He's at my house—Rachel Hollister's, I mean. Hurry!"

As soon as she released the transmit button she heard a scratchy reply. Help was on the way.

Should she do as she'd been told or relay that message to Jace? Surely, he wouldn't think of entering the garage with the stalker until he had backup.

But apparently he had. When she looked for him, he was nowhere to be seen.

The garage was dimly lit by the car's headlights but not completely dark. Jace went as far as the jagged opening, then changed his mind. If he entered through Rachel's kitchen, maybe he could catch the stalker by surprise. And as long as his car was blocking the drive and she was safely inside it, he didn't see much risk. His windows weren't as easily break-able as those of a civilian's car so even if she were attacked there, she'd be relatively secure.

The siren announcing the arrival of a second patrol unit bearing the sheriff decided him on his next move. Vaulting over the porch railing, he used the extra key he had left from changing the locks and entered the house. Thankfully, it was deserted, affirming his conclusion that Rachel's assailant was working alone.

He quickly made his way to the side door and found it locked. All he had to do, however, was release the mechanism in the knob in order to ease it open.

Since he had the dark house behind him and the headlights of the cars pointed at him, Jace could observe the interior of the garage fairly well. What he saw gave him cold chills. A figure dressed in black was hunched over next to the broken opening in the door and was holding a hammer raised to strike. If he, or anyone else, had poked his head through that hole it would have been bad news.

Just then he heard Harlan's voice. "Hands up and come out," the sheriff shouted.

Jace saw Harlan's body break the beam of light. So did the assailant. The hammer began its downward arc. Jace did the only thing he could do to save his boss. He fired.

Rachel screamed "Jace!" and started to run toward the garage. If the sheriff hadn't physically held her back she would have entered without thought for herself.

"Jace!"

"I'm okay. Harlan, call the medics, will you. We've got a wounded man here."

She continued struggling until she'd heard Jace's calm, as-sertive voice. Now, she sagged against the sheriff. "Praise God. He's all right."

"Sounds like it," Harlan said. "Can I trust you to stay out here till I get back?"

Rachel nodded, unable to catch her breath enough to speak again. Jace wasn't injured. It was amazing, given the circumstances. How had he gotten the best of the man in the garage? And who in the world was the assailant?

Just then, she looked up and gasped. There stood the love of her life, arm in arm with the man in black, helping him walk through the hole in the broken door and out into the driveway. When she recognized her stalker, she was thunderstruck.

"You know this guy?" Jace asked.

Rachel nodded. "Yes. That's Bud Foster. He's—he's one of the electricians who fixed the heater in the store. He works at the courthouse, too. Remember? No wonder he didn't have any trouble sneaking that card into the rack. I see him so often I barely paid any attention."

"That doesn't explain why he was so mad at you," Jace said. He gave the man's shoulder a shake and heard him moan.

"Watch it. I'm shot."

"Not badly," Jace said. "You have the right to remain silent. If you give up…"

Rachel listened to Jace read him his full Miranda rights, then say, "Okay. Talk. What did you have against Ms. Hollister? What did she ever do to you?"

The man coughed and winced before answering. "It's what she didn't do, not what she did. She thought she was too good to date me. Too high and mighty."

Astounded, Rachel scowled at him. "What are you talking about? I've never even spoken to you other than professionally or to say hello when we pass on the street."

"See?" Bud insisted, making a sour face at her.

"What made you think I wouldn't date you? You never even tried to ask me out."

"No, but George told me. He oughta know. He's your daddy." He eyed a familiar car that was pulling to a stop in front of the stakeout house. "There he is. Go ahead. Ask him."

Rachel sagged back against the scratched fender of her car. "My father again. I should have known. I think it's time he and I had a serious discussion about my love life. And this time, *I'm* going to do all the talking."

Jace handed his prisoner over to the sheriff and rejoined Rachel, taking her in his arms and holding tight. "What will you say?"

She cuddled closer before she answered. "You can listen to the whole conversation. As a matter of fact, I want you to. I plan to tell him that I've fallen in love with a cop and am no longer in the market for a husband."

Raising her face she studied the astonishment in Jace's expression. "If that's all right with you."

"It's more than all right. It's perfect," he said tenderly.

"Good, because I can't think of anyone I'd rather spend the rest of my life with than you, Deputy Morgan."

Tears of joy misted her vision. This was the answer to many of her prayers, all wrapped up in one wonderful man. And if she had not faced danger, they might never have gotten to know each other.

"Will you do me one favor?" Rachel asked.

"Kiss you, before your father gets here and starts hollering at everybody? We'd better hurry. He looks fit to be tied."

"I was thinking of something else. Will you be sure to give me a really pretty Valentine in a few days? I want to remember this holiday fondly for the rest of my life, not have it spoiled because of some guy who isn't rowing his boat with both oars in the water."

"Gladly," Jace said, grinning. "Know where I can find a lacy, expensive card?"

"I think so. And when you go to buy it, be sure to tell Eloise who it's for. It'll make her day."

Jace wasn't surprised when Rachel pivoted to address her red-faced father with a casual "Hi, Dad." What did astonish him was the calm way she stood her ground.

"Will somebody please explain what's going on?" George demanded.

"Gladly," she said, "but you're not going to like what you hear."

Jace felt George's piercing stare settle on him. "Are you going to tell me *he's* involved?"

"For the rest of my life, if I get my way," she said, tightening one arm around Jace's waist and leaning closer, much to his relief. "And that's just the beginning. Maybe you'd better sit down, Dad."

Grinning, Jace couldn't resist adding, "Yeah, *Dad*. Sitting is an excellent idea. Rachel and I have plenty to tell you and I'd hate to have you fall over in a faint when you find out what apparently triggered her stalker in the first place."

Rachel touched her father's hand and said, "I think he knows. Don't you, Dad?"

The color left the older man's face as he stared at the familiar person the sheriff was loading into his car. "It was Bud?"

"Yes." Jace kept her close, protecting her from the danger that no longer existed because it gave him a sense of tranquility to do so. "He was under the impression that you had tried to set up a date for him with Rachel and that she had refused."

The starch seemed to go out of George and he shook his head sadly. "It wasn't like that. I didn't think he was right for her so I kept making excuses whenever he approached me about it."

"Well, in that case you were right," Jace said. He gave his future bride a squeeze. "Now, what do you think about me? Will I do? Because I think our Rachel has made up her mind and I'd like your blessing."

"You're a *cop*." George's eyebrows arched.

Rachel laughed and cast a loving gaze at Jace that melted his heart as she said, "I know, Dad. I know. But nobody's perfect."

EPILOGUE

One of the things that gave Rachel the biggest thrill was the way her father had mellowed in the aftermath of the stalker incident. George wasn't a totally different man. That would have been too much to hope for. But he was definitely easier to get along with. She had been wondering if the changes were all in her imagination until her mother, Ruth, finally broached the subject.

Standing in an anteroom of Serenity Chapel, awaiting her entrance as a bride, Rachel beamed and clasped Ruth's slim hands. "I'm so glad you mentioned that, Mom. I've thought Dad was acting much better, too."

"It was enough of a change to impress me," her mother said, growing teary-eyed. "I was just about at the end of my rope with that man."

"I know what you mean. Jace is kind of like Dad in some ways, only he values my opinion. That's the biggest difference I can see." She giggled. "That, and he's a whole lot handsomer."

Ruth's smile was tender and filled with understanding. "And that's the way it should be. You should always look at your husband as if he is the most attractive man you've ever seen." She sighed. "There was a time when I looked at your father that way."

Rachel was concerned. "You don't now?"

"I hadn't for years. Not until recently." She gave her

daughter a brief hug and smiled through misty eyes. "Maybe I just needed you and Jace to remind me how it could be. How it should be between a husband and wife."

"It is scary to think of committing my whole life to him," Rachel admitted, "but I can't imagine not having him with me forever."

"And *that* is the best sign of all."

"It still frightens me to know he's putting himself in harm's way so often. How did you deal with that when Dad was working and was gone so much?"

"I shut him out," Ruth admitted, sobering. "I can see now that it was wrong but it was my way of sheltering myself from the loss I was sure I'd eventually experience." She began to smile again. "But, as you can see, he's still very much alive and kicking."

"That's like something Pastor Logan told Jace and me during counseling. We have to trust God and take one day at a time. If we borrow trouble it's like saying that we only believe selected parts of the Bible, the ones that fit our preconceived notions."

The door opened and Becky Malloy, the matron of honor, stuck her head in. "Hey, you two. Let's get this show on the road. It's time for everyone else to be seated and Logan doesn't want the groom to keel over because he had to wait too long."

Rachel laughed lightly. "Jace? Keel over? I doubt that very much. He's faced a lot worse trials than getting married."

That comment was apparently funnier than Rachel thought because it made Becky laugh aloud. She took Ruth's hand and led her from the room, leaving Rachel to pick up her bouquet of white and pink roses and follow.

If Jace really was nervous then maybe it was okay for her insides to be quaking and her hands to be clammy, Rachel reasoned. They were taking a big step. Together. If she had not been on her way to meet Jace and take her place by his side, she might have turned and run.

The way I fled from my stalker, she added to her thoughts with a shiver. It was good to know that the poor deluded man was institutionalized but there was still an element of fear that occasionally crept into her thoughts and left her unnecessarily breathless.

"For God has not given us the spirit of fear; but of power, and of love, and of a sound mind," she whispered, quoting her favorite verse from II *Timothy*.

She stepped into place at the head of the center aisle as soon as she got the signal and waited while Becky led the way forward. The sanctuary was packed. Cascades of fresh flowers decorated the altar. The organ music swelled.

For a second, Rachel wished she had not opted to walk alone rather than let her father be her escort. When Jace had suggested that George stand up for him as his best man, she had readily agreed. Anything that brought her father and her future husband together was fine with her.

Now, however, her knees felt weak and she wished she had someone's strong arm to lean on. She smiled to herself. On the way back, as Mrs. Jace Morgan, she would have.

She raised her eyes. There he was! Jace. More handsome than ever, so captivating she could hardly contain her joy. And, as his gaze met hers, Rachel was no longer alone.

He smiled tenderly, his very presence calling out to her.

Grinning through happy tears, she took one step forward, then another. The cadence of the customary music was far too slow to suit her. Her soft veil fluttered against her cheeks and the fabric of her full skirt rustled as she picked up the pace.

Jace began to beam. He held out his hand to her. As soon as her fingers touched his, he said, "I thought you'd never get here."

"Neither did I," she replied softly. "But now that I'm here…"

Logan Malloy cleared his throat noisily, making Rachel blush.

She held tightly to Jace's hand as the ceremony—and the rest of her life—began.

* * * * *

Dear Reader,

I was thrilled to be asked to write this novella. Every new project is a challenge and I love figuring out ways to tell a great story and share my faith at the same time. It's not always easy but it is rewarding.

This time, I began with *Psalms* 34:4, "I sought the Lord and He answered me; He delivered me from all my fears." By the time I had helped Rachel and Jace struggle through to the end, I was struck by a different verse in II *Timothy* 1:7. "For God has not given us a spirit of fear; but of power and of love and of a sound mind." In a way, as my characters' faith grew and blossomed, so did mine. I pray that yours will, too. All you have to do is call out to the Lord and He will accept you, just as you are.

I love to hear from my readers. The easiest way to reach me is by e-mail, val@valeriehansen.com or send a letter to P.O. Box 13, Glencoe, AR 72539. You can also see my other work at valeriehansen.com.

Blessings,

Valerie Hansen

QUESTIONS FOR DISCUSSION

1. Rachel feels safe because she lives in a small town. Is that a logical conclusion? Why or why not?

2. Jace has left his former job on a big city police department and come to Serenity to escape his past. Does his geographical location really matter or is he fooling himself?

3. Rachel's father means well. Why can't he see that he's actually hurting her? Or, do you feel he's doing the right thing because it's for her benefit?

4. When Eloise decides to turn the business over to Rachel and make her a partner, she's giving away a lot. Have you ever known anyone who is really that altruistic? Would you suspect them of having ulterior motives if something similar happened to you?

5. The person who is stalking Rachel is able to make himself seem normal and unimportant. Isn't that what makes him so scary?

6. Rachel has a strong bias against law enforcement officers. What if she was never able to overcome that preconceived notion? Look what she would miss! Has God ever had to use others or circumstances to bring about a positive change in your life? Are you glad?

Dedicated to my writing buddies and fellow brainstormers for this story: Linda Gilden, Candy Arrington and Missy Tippens. The retreat at the beach was awesome! Can't wait until next year.

A big thank-you goes to my wonderfully talented editor, Emily Rodmell. Thanks for giving me the opportunity to do this!

And as always, thank you to Jesus for letting me write.

Trust in the Lord with all your heart and lean not on your own understanding; in all your ways acknowledge him and he will make your paths straight.

—Proverbs 3:5–6

ONE

She'd been robbed!

A scream ripped from Holly Maddox's throat as receding footsteps beat in time with the radiating pain in her head.

Touching her forehead, she felt the warm wetness seep between her fingers.

Eyes squinting against the pulsing throb, she stumbled to the door—and ran into what felt like a slab of concrete. She felt another scream building when warm hands cupped her shoulders and the voice she still heard in her dreams said, "Holly, it's me. What happened?"

"Eli?" She choked down the hysteria as he led her back inside to sit on a stool. She heard running water then felt a cool cloth cover the gash she figured she had on her forehead. However, her mind suddenly wasn't on the break-in or her throbbing head. It was on the unexpected appearance of a man she hadn't seen in almost six years. With no contact for more than half a decade, why did he have to choose this moment to come back? She'd dreamed that if she ever saw her ex-boyfriend again she'd be looking great to show him what he lost, not standing in her store, bleeding after being robbed and clubbed in the head.

"I've called the police," his voice soothed. "An ambulance is on the way, too."

"I don't need an ambulance. Cancel it, will you?" In shock, she asked, "What are you doing here?"

In spite of the pain, she couldn't take her eyes from him. She'd heard he was back in town, on leave from the police force in New York to take care of his injured father. Holly had gone out of her way to make sure their paths didn't cross on his previous visits home for holidays and vacations. Looked like she hadn't been careful enough this time.

Grudgingly, she admitted he looked as good as ever with his silky dark hair and green eyes. Anger thrummed through her. Well, she wouldn't fall for him again, that was for sure. He'd broken her heart twice, once when he'd left to go away to college. After that and the police academy, he'd moved home to work as a deputy with the police department. They had resumed their relationship and she'd been thrilled. Until six months later, when he'd left for New York to become a detective.

She tuned back in to what he was saying. "I was on my way to get some groceries next door when I heard something crash and you scream."

A knock on the door interrupted and Holly dragged her gaze from Eli's rugged face. A face that used to inspire poetry, conjuring visions of a white dress and a tropical island honeymoon.

"What's going on in here?"

She winced.

Alex Harwood, sheriff of Rose Mountain. A more recent ex-boyfriend. A good guy with a soft spot for Holly. A very persistent soft spot. He was determined to convince her that their break-up was a mistake. She'd been on the fence, unable to decide—until right now.

Seeing Eli brought back old memories, old feelings—and old hurt. She wasn't ready to date anyone at this point in time. But letting Alex know that would have to wait.

Even though Alex was the sheriff with deputies who patrolled the town, he always said it was his town and he'd work the streets until he was kicked off them. And the fact that it was Holly in trouble had been enough to bring him running.

Holly heard Eli explain what he'd witnessed, then it was her turn. She looked up into Alex's blue gaze and wondered what went on behind them. One of the reasons she'd decided they were wrong for each other. She couldn't get a good read on him.

Eli squeezed her hand. "Hey, are you in there? Tell Alex what happened."

Sucking in a fortifying breath, she said, "Jessica Horn, my part-time worker, left about an hour ago. I closed up shop and came back here to finish paying some bills. The next thing I know, someone's in the store with me."

"You didn't have the alarm on?"

She shook her head and groaned. Wrong move. She waited for the pain to subside. "No, I always set it when I leave, but rarely do it while I'm here. Guess I will from now on," she muttered. "Anyway, when I turned to see who had come through the door, I came face-to-face with my metal trash can." She pointed to the object lying on the floor where it had landed after contact with her head.

"Pretty confident crook, wasn't he? To come in here while she was here." Eli interjected toward Alex. "Wonder why he didn't wait for her to leave?"

Alex shrugged. "I don't know. Like you said, gutsy. Or maybe desperate. If he came in with her here, he didn't have to worry about finding a way in past locks and an alarm system." He shut the notebook he'd taken notes in. "What did the guy take?"

"The bank's bag of checks and cash I had sitting on the edge of the desk. I was too late to get to the bank today so I was going to take it home with me then drop it by on my way in tomorrow morning." Money wasn't so tight she was desperate, but losing a whole day's worth of profits would hurt. "It was about a thousand dollars all total. Not a huge amount, but…" she shrugged.

Alex nodded, his blue eyes tracking her. "We don't have a big drug problem in this town, but I'll check around and see if I can find out anything." He looked at Eli then Eli's hand where it rested on her shoulder and gave a flicker of a frown. She hadn't realized it was there. Standing up dislodged the weight of it and, with chagrin, she realized she missed it. She'd plain missed *him*.

Disgusted with herself for feeling that small smidge of attraction for the man in the midst of everything that was happening, not to mention everything he'd done in the past, she led Alex into the next room of her store. The Candy Caper. Her pride and joy—and source of income. She'd always had a weakness for chocolate and a head for business. After scraping together her business degree, the store seemed the perfect fit for her. She'd opened the town's only gourmet candy store with a special section that focused on chocolate only. It had been an instant hit with the town folks and had even been written up in a number of tourist magazines. Boxes of candy, red and pink balloons, stuffed animals and fresh flowers all waited to be delivered to their lucky Valentine recipients. The ice cream case next to the wall gleamed. "Nothing seems to be disturbed in here."

"All right. I'll take care of dusting the back room for prints, but don't expect much. Did the guy have on gloves or did you notice?"

She closed her eyes trying to remember the last thing her eyes had seen before she'd been hit. "Yes, he had on black gloves."

"Did you see his face?" Eli asked.

"No, a glimpse of a mask and gloves, but that's it." She rummaged in her drawer for a bottle of ibuprofen and shot a look at Eli. "Did you cancel that ambulance?"

Alex narrowed his eyes. "You sure you want to do that?"

She squinted right back at him. Persistent and overprotective. "I'm sure. It's a small cut. Head wounds usually look worse than they are." Or so she'd heard.

Eli took her chin and tilted it for a look at the damage. Her heart jumped into triple speed. "I canceled it." His warm breath brushed her cheek, then he stepped back. Holly fought to catch her breath as he headed for the door. "I'm just going to have a look outside."

When he left, Alex stared at her like he wanted to say something and couldn't decide whether or not he should. Not in the mood for either man, dismayed at her instant response to a man who'd pulverized her heart, she just wanted everyone gone so she could put an ice pack on her head. "Is that everything you need?"

A slow smile crossed his lips. "Not everything, but I have your number if I have any more questions. Although I can think of one question I'd like to ask you. It involves a ring."

Holly frowned. "Alex…" she gently reproved.

He shrugged and offered a sheepish grin. "Can't blame a guy for trying. You know I'm crazy about you, Holly."

"Stop it, will you?"

Alex just kept that goofy smile on his face. She wondered if he was even thinking about the break-in. "I'll just get out of your way so you can do your job."

A gentle hint.

Eli came back in and Holly watched Alex's expression slide from personal back to professional. Eli asked, "Are you sure you don't want me to run you up to the E.R. in Bryson City?"

A thirty-minute drive away, the small town had the closest hospital. "No, I'm fine. Between the ice and the ibuprofen, I'll survive. I don't think he got me hard enough to cause a concussion, but if I start feeling sick, I'll call for help."

"All right." He hesitated in the door and looked like he wanted to say something else, then sighed. He looked at Alex then back at her. "Did you notice anything off when you came in the store?"

She frowned. "Off? What do you mean?"

"Just odd, anyone standing outside, looking like they didn't belong. A feeling of being watched. Anything like that?"

Holly shrugged. "No." A sigh escaped her. "I guess I need

to be a little more alert about my surroundings." A memory hit her. "Wait a minute. There was something...."

Both Alex and Eli jumped in and chorused, "What?"

"There was someone standing across the street smoking a cigarette. I remember thinking he was new in town, but then I came on in and got involved in everything here—" she waved a hand toward her desk "—and didn't think anything more about him until just now." Normally, Holly tried to introduce herself to any newcomers, explain who she was and tell them about the store. But she'd been in a hurry today, just wanting to get things done and get home.

Alex nodded. "We've had a few visitors in town lately because of the auction coming up, but I'll check it out." Although the town had its usual share of tourists during the summer and fall months, in February it became a ghost town for all intents and purposes. Strangers during the winter season stood out.

Eli shifted toward the door. "I guess I'll go get my groceries."

"I'll see that you get home safely, Holly," Alex offered.

Holly hesitated. Did she really want to allow him to do that when she knew she was going to have to convince him she wasn't the girl for him?

Eli, as much as he'd hurt her in the past, was definitely the better choice for an escort this time. "Um, actually, I think I need to get a few things, too. Eli, I'll just walk on over with you."

Surprise brightened his green gaze and he held the door for her. She turned back to Alex as she passed in front of Eli. "Call me when you're done and I'll come back and set the alarm."

Without giving either man a chance to respond, she exited the building, Eli following behind.

It had been all Eli could do to suppress his cop instincts. Everything in him had wanted to jump in and process the scene.

But he'd resisted. He wasn't a cop in this town anymore and investigating the incident at Holly's store wasn't his right. But he wasn't blind, either. Something was going on between Holly and the sheriff. The thought made his heart cramp. "Hey. Are you sure you're all right?"

"I'm sure."

"Okay." He didn't want to ask, but he had to know. "What's going on with you and Alex?"

She stopped just outside the entrance to the grocery store. "What do you mean?"

"Oh come on, Holly. You guys had vibes going all over the place. Are you two an item?"

"No!"

He couldn't help the relief he felt at her vehement response. "Okay, then what?"

She took a deep breath like she might launch into telling him then shook her head. "Not that it's any of your business, but we dated. I called it off and he didn't want it to end. He's been after me to get back together with him."

"Ah." A pause. "So why did you call it off?"

"Because it just wasn't right. I wanted it to be, but…" Her look singed him. Was *he* the reason it hadn't been right with Alex? He sure hoped so. She continued, "He says I didn't give him a fair shot at winning my heart—or some nonsense." She rubbed her head. He was sure it ached and that she was probably ready to get home. Her next words confirmed that. "So, now I guess I'd better get in here and get a few groceries then get home to Mom."

Worry wrinkled the skin of her forehead. He wanted to smooth it out for her. "How is your mother? My dad said she was doing chemo and radiation again."

"Yeah, the cancer came back. She just finished another round. We're waiting on the report to see if they got it all again."

"Aw, Holly, I'm so sorry."

Tears filled her eyes and she blinked them back, but not

before one slipped down her cheek. As though it had a will of its own, his finger came up to catch the drop before it could fall. Her breath sucked in at the touch and he wondered if she felt the same tingle of awareness that he did.

That same awareness that had first drawn him to her when they'd both been sophomores in high school.

With a jerky movement, she shoved the door open. "I'm just going to get my stuff and get going. Alex should be done pretty soon."

Gladness filled him. Yeah, she felt it. So, she was still attracted to him. Hope that he might win her forgiveness, her trust and possibly her friendship nearly made him lightheaded. But just because they still had that special bit of chemistry between them didn't mean she'd be willing to do anything about it. He still had a lot to prove to her. "I'll wait for you and follow you home."

The protest he expected hovered on her lips, but then her eyes slid in the direction of her store and she swallowed, nodded. Twice in one night she'd been willing to accept his help, spend time in his presence. What could that possibly mean?

Twenty minutes later, they were done, Alex was gone, her alarm was set, and she was in her car, heading up the mountain. Eli followed a few yards back, his heart beating hard against his chest.

He'd come home to help with his father and make things right with Holly. Today had been a start. When she turned left onto the long drive that led to her house, a prayer whispered through him.

Lord, I'm so new at this. Please continue to help me know what to say and what to do. I'm a different person than I was six years ago, but You and I are the only ones who know it right now. Give me the opportunity to apologize to Holly. And maybe the chance to show her I'm trustworthy now and see if there's anything left to build a relationship on. I know it'll take time. Help me be patient.

His prayer trailed off as he pulled into his drive. Buckeye's truck sat in the spot where he'd parked this morning. A good and faithful friend was hard to find but his dad had one in Stan Buck, or Buckeye to everyone who knew him.

Eli would make sure there was a little something extra in the man's paycheck this week even though he knew Buckeye didn't expect that. He also knew Buckeye had a single daughter with a baby on the way. A lot of the man's check went to help with her medical expenses.

Entering the house, Eli noted the scent of roast and rolls still lingered in the air and knew he'd find some leftovers in the fridge.

Miz Hannah had been the family cook since Eli was two. She'd been like a grandmother to him and was as much a part of the family as Eli himself. When he was twelve, and his mother had taken off to parts unknown, Hannah had smothered him with as much love as he could stand.

And when they'd been teenagers, Holly had been in and out of this house almost on a daily basis.

Then he'd left and broken her heart.

And he'd been too self-centered to worry about it. Regret pierced him. He'd always justified leaving by telling himself that he'd asked her to go with him and she'd refused. Now, he realized just how selfish he'd been to expect her to leave her sick mother and follow after him…and his dreams.

"Dad?" Eli entered the den and found his father sitting in his wheelchair, he and Buckeye watching a preseason baseball game on the big-screen television. His outstretched casted leg hung from the traction device designed to keep the limb as immobile as possible.

Eli flopped onto the couch beside Buckeye. "Who's winning?"

"It's tied right now."

For the next half hour, Eli cheered and groaned according to his team's performance, enjoying the evening with his dad.

TWO

With a trembling hand, Holly hung up the phone and went back to the window to push the curtain aside a millimeter. Duster, her beloved German shepherd, whined at her side and Sassy, a shy border collie, yipped at the door.

After taking some nausea medicine, her mother had finally fallen asleep. Needing the distraction from her constant replaying in her mind of the assault, Holly had planned to go over her personal bills. She'd just settled at the table to work when she heard a noise outside.

She'd jumped, startled. A little uneasy. Then she'd laughed at herself and decided she was still jumpy after her ordeal at the shop. Then she'd heard it again and noticed the dogs were restless. When she'd looked out the window, a shadow had passed by.

She'd dialed 9-1-1 then hung up before it even rang. What if someone wasn't out there, and it was just her overactive imagination and on-edge nerves due to the break-in at her store? And she really didn't want to deal with Alex again. But if someone really was skulking around outside and she needed help...

So she'd called Eli.

Did he still carry a gun?

Another rattle against her back door. Her stomach dropped to her toes only to bounce back up into her throat. *Oh, Lord, please...*

Duster's ears went flat against his head. Sassy had disappeared. All she had to do was tell Duster to "dust it up, boy" and he'd go after whatever she pointed at. But she couldn't do that yet.

A weapon. She needed a weapon. She had her mother to protect. Avoiding the windows as much as possible, she skirted her way into the kitchen. The block of knives sat by the sink.

Could she actually use one on somebody?

Shaking fingers reached out to grasp the handle of the largest one. She pulled it from its sheath without a sound. The lone kitchen light over the sink glinted off the blade and Holly swallowed hard.

Turning back toward the door, she paused, knife held aloft, ready to do some damage to whomever dared to try and get past her locked kitchen door.

Scrape, thud.

Duster barked and Holly shushed him. She didn't think he'd scare away the intruder, and his barking might wake her mother. Holly didn't need that right now.

Screech!

She jumped again and heard the blood rushing in her ears. Whoever was out there wasn't being very careful. What if the shadow had been a figment of her imagination? What if the sound was just an animal? A raccoon looking for a late-night snack? Her adrenaline eased.

The pounding of her heart slowed and her fingers loosened their grip a fraction. Moving to the back door, she tested the knob. Locked. Her ears strained to hear, desperate for advance notice of impending danger.

Duster paced the floor and whined. Someone, something, was definitely out there.

The police force in Rose Mountain consisted of five deputies and a sheriff. If she called 9-1-1 again, what were the odds Alex would come? If he was listening to the scanner, he'd insist on taking the call.

So what? He was the sheriff. She was scared enough right now, she'd welcome him. She started to dial.

Hesitated.

Or was she just being overly jumpy because of the store incident? Speaking of which, did this have anything to do with that? Did the person think he'd find more money or whatever at her home?

Hands trembling, heart thudding, she wondered what she should do. One hand clutched the knife, the other the phone. Her finger hovered over the one.

She didn't want to cry wolf, and yet...

Listening, she strained to hear anything.

Nothing.

Things had quieted down outside, but Duster kept his ears pricked toward the window.

During a quick glance around the kitchen, the blinds on one window caught her attention. They gaped, exposing the blackness beyond. She shuddered, feeling creeped out by the night and all the noises it brought with it.

Deciding she'd been foolish and would owe Eli an apology for calling him out here, she hung up and went to close the blinds.

Just as she reached up to pull the string that would snap them shut, a face in a mask popped up to eye level then jerked back as though surprised to see her. Her heart leaped and her stomach dropped as terror shot its way through her veins.

As quickly as the face appeared it was gone. Through sheer willpower, she swallowed the scream pounding for release and yanked the blinds shut.

Whirling from the window, she raced to the wall and started flipping on all of the outside lights. The hand still clutching the knife knocked a canister to the kitchen floor. She ignored it.

Tires crunched on the gravel outside and she froze.

Eli? It had to be.

She edged to the back door and pushed aside the curtain

covering the window. Eli's truck. And he was about to climb out with a prowler nearby.

Holly opened the door, pointed in the direction she'd last heard the intruder and said, "Dust it up, boy." The dog bounded out, barking furiously. He disappeared around the side of the house. Seconds later, the faint sound of a motorcycle reached her ears.

Eli bolted from his car, ran across the lawn and followed after Duster.

Ten minutes later, Eli gave up the search. He and Duster made their way back to the house where Holly stood on the porch, knife in hand.

He motioned to it. "I think you can put that away now."

She stared at him blankly, then looked down at her hand. "Oh." She looked surprised to see the weapon. "When I thought... I had to grab something..."

He'd seen this before. Mild shock.

Carefully, he approached her. "Give me the knife, Holly. You're safe."

With a hand that still shook with fine tremors, she handed the knife over to him.

He placed an arm around her shoulders and led her into the house. Duster skirted around them and made his way over to the rug in front of the fireplace. Another animal appeared from the back of the house and followed Duster's example. Eli smiled. "Still taking in strays, I see."

Holly's shoulders stiffened and she pulled away from him. "Of course."

The shock was wearing off. "I'll just put this back in the kitchen for you. If you have a powerful flashlight, I can take a look around. You might want to call Alex, too."

"I know. If someone was really out there, then I suppose that's what I need to do. I'll think about it."

Confused, he just looked at her.

Her expression softened. "Sorry, but Alex is—" She paused

and waved a hand in the air as though searching for the right word. She finally settled on "not the person I want to call."

"But he's the sheriff. He needs to know."

"I know, but I don't want to encourage him if I don't have to. If I go running to him with this…" She sighed. "Please, I'd rather handle this on my own."

That rocked him back for a minute. She didn't want to call Alex because the man was still after her to reunite. He wondered what she'd say if he offered her his help. "I'm going to go have a look around and then we're going to have a talk. All right?"

She raised a hand to rub the side of her head that wasn't bruised. "Look, I'm probably just being paranoid. Most likely, this was all just some stupid prank or something…."

"Like the break-in at your shop?"

That took the wind from her sails. "I don't know what to think, Eli."

"Get me that light. I'll be back in a minute."

"Okay."

She set off to find the light. Returning, she handed it to him, looked deep into his eyes for a brief moment before saying, "Thanks."

He nodded and walked to the door. Flipping the light on, he headed to where the motorcycle had disappeared. Since Holly hadn't heard the approach, whoever had been on the motorcycle had probably walked it up to the house.

The light pierced the darkness, but revealed nothing as to the identity of the man on the motorcycle.

When he returned to the house, Holly had a cup of coffee in one hand, her fingers drumming the side of the mug in nervous taps.

"I didn't see anything. Sorry."

She blew out a harsh sigh. "Thanks for looking."

"No problem." He handed her the light.

Hesitating at the door, she finally seemed to make up her mind about something. "You want to come in?"

"I want you to tell me who you think might have been lurking outside your house."

"I have no idea." She waved her empty hand. "I don't have anything of any real value except Mom's silver and china. The usual stuff. But other than that…"

"All right, well you need to keep your doors locked, that's for sure. Someone's targeted you for some reason." He paused. "You said Alex was constantly harassing you about getting back with him. Could he have been out here doing a little spying on you?"

Biting her lip, she studied her mug. "I don't think so. Alex is the sheriff, he's harmless. Persistent, but harmless. He's more into sending me gifts than scaring me."

"What kind of gifts?"

"Expensive ones. First it was flowers at my shop. Then today I got—" she set her mug on the end table, crossed the room and opened a drawer "—this."

She dropped a box in his outstretched hand.

He opened it and whistled.

"Tell me about it." She shook her head and rolled her eyes. "For the auction, he even signed up to be on the same committee as I am." She flushed. "That sounds really egotistical, doesn't it?" Throwing up her hands, she said, "I don't know. It's just when sign-ups went around at church for the auction…" She shrugged.

His dad had explained it to him the last time Eli had been home. The church had come up with the idea for the auction after a mission trip to Haiti two years ago. Holly had been a part of that trip and had fallen in love with the children of the orphanage they'd worked with. On their last day, they'd learned that the place was on the brink of being shut down. When the team had returned to America, the church voted to do what they could to help and had come up with the idea of an auction. Anything donated was auctioned off. To Eli, it looked like a huge yard sale, only in auction format. It had been so successful, they'd made it an annual event.

And the orphanage thrived. His dad also said Holly planned to go back sometime in the summer. He tried to picture what he would be doing four months from now. Briefly, the interview for the job as captain of the New York precinct flashed through his mind. He still hadn't heard anything about that and had just about given up on it.

"Holly?"

Lashes fanned her cheeks as she closed her eyes for a brief moment. She opened them. "Mom? We're in here."

At the sight of Holly's mother, Eli's breath left him. A mere shadow of the woman he remembered from his youth and even six years ago, she was now wasted away from her illness. No wonder Holly was so adamant about sticking around and taking care of her. Just like she had right after her dad died and cancer struck Mrs. Maddox, in Holly's senior year of high school.

Holly watched Eli cross the room to give her mom a gentle hug. Her mother patted his arm and then held on to it as he led her to the couch. She settled down and said, "I heard voices."

Holly covered her mother with an afghan from the back of the couch. "We were just discussing Alex."

"Ah. A very persistent young man, isn't he? It's a shame you two didn't suit each other." She shifted into a more comfortable position then snapped her eyes to Holly. "Oh, speaking of persistent, I almost forgot to tell you that the nice man from the real estate office, Mr. Miller, came by today with Jarrod Parker."

"What nice man? And why was our lawyer with him?"

Forehead wrinkled in thought, Holly's mother said, "You know, the one who came by last week. You weren't here, but I told you about him." She looked at Eli. "He wants to buy this place."

"What did you tell him?" Holly heard the sharpness in her voice, but couldn't help it. She was so tired of dealing with these people. Why was it no one could seem to take no for an answer anymore?

"I told him we would discuss it."

Patience, Holly. "There's nothing to discuss, Mom. This is my childhood home, the place Daddy poured sweat, blood and tears into. How can you just give it up so easily?"

Her mother laughed, "Oh, honey, it's just a house. Yes, we had some good times here, but it's time to move on. Your life would be so much easier if you didn't have to worry about taking care of this place."

"I don't mind." Holly crossed her arms, body language shouting her resistance. "Besides, I have help. Mr. Ryan has been here for years. What would he do if we sold this place out from under him?" Holly's father had hired Will Ryan when Holly was in the third grade. The man loved this place as much as she did, although he kept a small apartment in town. "And what was Mr. Parker doing with the man from the real estate company anyway?"

Her mother frowned. "Will Ryan needs to retire. The poor man is getting older and can't keep up like he used to. That's why he only puts in a few hours a day. And don't let him fool you, he's got a nice little nest egg squirreled away and can very easily quit working. He only stays on because he knows you need the help." She flicked a hand. "As for Mr. Miller, it seems like I might have mentioned that our lawyer handled everything. I guess he went to Jarrod, who, by the way—" she eyed Holly sternly "—thinks it would be a wise move."

"Why that sneaking, conniving, land-hungry…" Her fingernails dug into her palms as she clenched her fists. But part of her digested her mother's words about Mr. Ryan. He only stayed on to help her? She thought it was because he couldn't bring himself to quit working. Guilt stabbed her.

Eli held up a hand. "Um, I think I'll just head on home." He looked at Holly. "Are you okay with that?"

She paused midtirade and flushed. "Yes, of course. Sorry, I'm just a little stressed right now."

"Don't you want to report what happened—"

"Um, no," she broke in, eyes flashing a warning about discussing this in front of her mother.

He got the message and bit his tongue. He obviously didn't agree with her, but at least he didn't say anything more. "All right. I guess I'll see you tomorrow."

"You will?"

"Elva Sharp called, said you told her you would pick up her stuff for the auction and thought you would need help. Apparently my dad volunteered me when she came to visit him in the hospital a couple of weeks ago. She called this morning to let me know."

Holly was in charge of collecting the "treasures" to be auctioned off. She groaned. "I'd forgotten all about that."

"I'll be by to pick you up after lunch, all right?"

Her smile felt weak. "Right."

He left and Holly turned to see that her mother had slipped back into a doze. Not bothering to get her to move to her bed, Holly tucked the blanket a little tighter then checked all the doors once more.

Moving to the window where she'd seen the masked man shortly before, she tilted an eye-level blind and looked out at the darkness. Her stomach rolled with remembered fear.

Who had it been? Why was someone so intent on either scaring her or robbing her? Were the incidents at the store and the one here at home related? Or were they just mere coincidence?

Too many questions and not enough answers.

Holly flipped the blind closed and sighed, wondering if she'd get any sleep at all—in spite of the exhaustion dragging through her and the aching throb pounding in her head.

However the night went, sleep or no sleep, she'd leave the floodlights on tonight.

THREE

As the sun finally made an appearance to Eli's left, the morning was as beautiful as all the ones he had remembered growing up. The barn lay straight ahead, rolling hills backdrop to the red-and-white structure. Picture perfect. He'd missed it more than he ever thought he would.

He reached the barn and climbed down from the saddle to hand the reins over to Buckeye. "Thanks. He's responding great. I think he's ready to sell along with the other two."

The horse snorted as Buckeye patted his neck. "So, you still remember how to break a horse even after all these years?"

"I was breaking horses before I could walk." Eli smiled at the gray-bearded man who'd worked on the ranch ever since Eli could remember.

Buckeye laughed then cleared his throat. "I know that boy. I was the one that taught you." Buckeye turned serious. "Your daddy needs you to take over this farm, Eli."

Eli studied the man. "I'll keep it running until Dad's back on his feet, but after that…"

"Well, whatever you decide, it's good to have you home."

Eli sucked in a lungful of the fresh mountain night air. "It's good to be here."

"You gonna miss being a big-city detective?"

Would he? Maybe parts of it. Definitely not other parts. He

shrugged. "I don't think so, Buckeye. I had my reasons for taking a leave of absence." Caring for his father was only one of them.

"Reasons you ain't sharing, huh?"

Eli shot the old man a look and turned his attention to digging his keys out of his pocket. "Guess I'll head on into town. I need to pick up a few things I didn't have time to get last night." He looked at his watch.

Plus, he wanted to check on Holly. After her crazy evening last night, he hoped she got some rest. She hadn't called again so he assumed the remainder of her night had been peaceful. He patted the horse's neck. "Working with Stargazer here took me a lot longer than I'd planned."

"When's your dad's next doctor's appointment?"

"Tomorrow morning."

"He busted that leg up pretty good." Eli's father, Mitch Brodie, was too stubborn to admit he was too old to be competing in the rodeo. Two weeks ago, he'd been bucked off a grumpy bull. It certainly hadn't been the first time, but it had been one of the most painful. The bull's hoof had come down hard on Mitch's femur and broke it before the clowns were able to distract the angry animal. "One day your daddy's going to admit he's an old man."

"He's only forty-eight years old, Buckeye. That's looking younger every year to me."

Buckeye laughed again. "You're what? Twenty-eight? I remember the day you were born. Don't tell me what looks young."

Eli grinned. "Listen for Dad for me until I get back, will you?"

"You bet."

He left the horse in Buckeye's efficient care and headed for the house. After a quick shower, he popped his head in the den to find his dad in his wheelchair grumbling over a crossword puzzle. "Hey, I'll be back soon. Buckeye can help you with anything you need."

"I don't need a babysitter, you know."

"Right." He grinned and left knowing Buckeye would be along in a few minutes.

Eli climbed into his truck and made his way toward town. Four minutes later, he passed the turnoff to Holly Maddox's home. His mind went to her as it did every time he drove this way.

Holly. His high school sweetheart. The one girl he'd never forgotten. And he'd certainly tried.

When he'd said goodbye to her six years ago, he hadn't realized how much it would hurt. But it had been the right thing to do, he'd rationalized. After all, he had a career to think of. At least that's what he'd told himself. And when Holly had refused to go with him, he'd decided he didn't need her, that if she had loved him enough…

Eli grimaced. He'd been so full of himself. He'd thought if he broke up with her and moved off, she'd come chasing after him. When she hadn't, his ego had been badly bruised.

The way he'd treated her had been wrong. But he hoped to set that right sometime soon.

He spun the truck into the parking lot of John's General Store. A combination gas/grocery/general store, it had been in the same family for over a hundred and fifty years.

And next door was The Candy Caper.

No small red truck in front, but he knew she'd arrive before too long.

He wondered what she'd do if he waited so he could go over to speak—to apologize for being a jerk after high school—and beyond. Would she even be interested in listening?

So far, she'd been pretty mellow but she'd also had a rough day yesterday. She'd been thankful for his presence last night. But now that the danger was past, how would she react if he brought up their relationship as the topic of conversation?

Probably toss him out on his ear. Which he would deserve.

With a sigh, he glanced at his watch. Eight-thirty. Already

people meandered down the sidewalk, entering and exiting the line of shops.

On his way into the store, a flash of red caught his eye.

Holly's truck.

Pulling into the sheriff's office parking lot.

Holly sat in her truck tapping the steering wheel and debating what she needed to do. The two-story building in front of her boasted oversize wooden doors and tall windows with wide sills.

Bright and early, before she had to meet Eli to pick up the auction items, Holly had decided it was time to talk to Alex Harwood. She'd known for a while now that she needed to do this, however, she'd made excuses to delay the confrontation and that wasn't fair to Alex. She felt like she might be guilty of leading him on by keeping the gifts. It was time to set him straight.

Movement in her rearview mirror caught her eye. Jumpy and on high alert since last night, she inspected every car that crossed her path, determined to be ready if danger came knocking again.

A black sedan had just pulled into the parking lot of the grocery store. Eli's truck sat beside the gas pump.

Focusing back on the sedan, she thought she saw cigarette smoke curl from the window.

Who were those guys?

No time to worry about it right now.

She looked at the bag on the seat then back to the door of the sheriff's office. She grimaced. Confrontation wasn't high on her list of favorite things to do.

But the longer she kept the gifts, the longer he might hold out hope she'd consider dating him again. That she was just going through a phase and would eventually come around. And she definitely didn't want that.

After she'd told him she didn't want to see him anymore, he'd continued to ask her out. She'd turned him down, but hadn't been as blunt as she should have been.

Two weeks ago, the gifts started arriving and she had to admit, because she was lonely, wanted marriage and children, she'd thought about resuming the relationship. About settling for Mr. Good Enough. But soon realized that she just didn't have the feelings for Alex that she'd once had for Eli. And if she continued the relationship with Alex she'd be cheating him out of finding the one meant for him. Not to mention cheating herself. And now Eli was back, and her reaction to him last night brought everything into clear focus.

Alex wasn't the man for her.

Lord, what's happening to my life? First, Mom's cancer comes back, I'm being harassed about selling my childhood home and I'm going to have to hurt a nice man. I really need Your help, please?

Holly huffed a sigh and glanced at the clock. She'd been sitting in her truck for a full ten minutes.

Firming her jaw and gathering her courage, she grabbed the bag from the back and climbed out.

The jail might look like a place Barney Fife might work, but she knew the officers inside were all business. She had gone to school with four out of the five. Alex had been elected sheriff in the last election and so far had done a good job from all that she could tell.

She really hated to hurt his feelings, but couldn't continue letting him believe they might pick up their relationship. She'd been on the receiving end of that kind of hurt and had resolved a long time ago never to do that to someone else.

You're stalling, Holly. Get in there and give this stuff back to Alex, tell him thank you very much, but no thanks.

She made her way up the steps. Pushing open the door, she stepped inside to inhale the smell of strong coffee and disinfectant.

Alice Colby sat at the receptionist desk working on the computer.

"Hi, Alice." Holly shifted the small bag to her other hand. "I need to give this to Alex. Is he around?"

"Right back through there at his desk. Working on the burglary at your shop, he said."

"Thanks, I'll just walk this back there and give it to him."

"Go for it, girl." The woman wiggled her eyebrows. It was no secret Holly and Alex had gone out. The town had them practically married off before the first date had even been finished. Not bothering to set the record straight, Holly walked through the metal detector and headed back to find Alex.

It wasn't hard.

His desk was at the front of the large room. Four other desks sat along the permanent walls, separated by five-foot-high movable walls. A phone rang to her left; printers whirred. Conversation ceased at her entrance.

All eyes centered on her as she walked over to Alex's desk.

He looked up and smiled. And she felt nothing even remotely romantic toward him. Why? His eyes? Eli's warm green ones flashed through her mind and immediate guilt hit her. She wasn't doing this because of Eli.

Well, not completely.

"Hi, Alex." She looked around. She hadn't expected an audience. "Hi, Joel, Harlan, guys." They nodded their greetings and she looked back at Alex. "Um, is there somewhere we can talk privately?"

At her words, everyone suddenly had something to do. Joel and Harlan grabbed their keys. Joel said, "I'll be patrolling the north end of town, Harlan's got the south."

Alex nodded. "I'll be out there soon."

Joel shot a glance at Holly. "Hey, Leigh-Ann wants to know when you're going to give her a call."

Leigh-Ann, Holly's best friend since middle school and Joel's wife of two years. "Tell her I'll try to call her today."

The men disappeared and the other two deputies vanished behind their desks.

The room gave the appearance of being empty, but Holly knew she had other ears there. Keeping her voice low, she said, "Here."

She dropped the bag on Alex's desk.

He frowned. "What's this?"

"Your gifts."

The frown faded, but she saw his jaw clench. Hurt flashed in his eyes. "What do you want me to do with them?"

She kept her tone even. "They're very nice gifts and I'm sure the next girl you date is going to be thrilled with the fact that you care enough to go all out for her. But—" she took a deep breath "—we're just not right for each other, okay?"

He eyed her, storm clouds building in his eyes that suddenly looked more gray than blue, his hurt spilling over into his words. "What is it with you, Holly? I'm not good enough for you? Because you knew me before we went out. I mean, it's not like we haven't known each other for years."

She closed her eyes briefly. "It has nothing to do with being good enough or not good enough, Alex. It has to do with having things in common. I was very flattered when you asked me out and you'll be a great guy for some girl, just not me, okay?"

That said, she turned and did her best to walk calmly from the place instead of bolting into a run—which is what she wanted to do.

"Bye, Alice."

The woman's goodbye echoed behind her as she shoved open the heavy wooden door and stepped outside into the freezing cold. Shivering, she pulled her coat tighter around her neck and gripped her keys in a gloved hand.

A hand on her arm jerked her around and she nearly stumbled. "What?" The word squeaked out.

Dark eyes glared down at her.

Eli topped off the gas tank then replaced the nozzle in its handle. Pulling out a twenty, he handed it to the man behind the glass.

"How ya doing, Eli?"

"Doing all right, Mr. Pearson. How about yourself?"

"Could complain, but I won't."

The grizzled man laughed at his own words and Eli smiled. Nothing ever changed much in this town. A fact he found himself more and more grateful for each day.

He shook his head. A year ago, if someone had told him he'd be standing in this very spot, or living on his father's ranch, he'd have laughed himself silly.

"Let go of me!"

His head shot up and he spun on his heel to see Holly arguing with a man in front of the police station.

Eli's temperature shot up as he watched the stranger manhandle her. "Hey!"

His shout went unheard as Holly continued her struggle to get away from the hand that held her upper arm. Her foot kicked out and caught a shin. Eli heard the man swear then Holly was free and running for her car.

Eli raced after her. "Holly!" She either didn't hear him or ignored his shout as she jumped into her car and squealed away from the sheriff's office.

The man looked up and pinned Eli with a malevolent glare that made his skin crawl. But he'd dealt with scum like this before.

Eli came up beside him. "What do you think you're doing?"

"It's business and none of yours. Back off, Brodie, or you might find yourself in a heap of trouble."

Eli narrowed his eyes. "Who are you and how do you know my name?"

A finger in his chest pushed him back and made him reach for the weapon he hadn't put on this morning. Dropping his hand, he held on to his temper.

"Keep your nose where it belongs. Put it in my business again and you'll be behind bars."

Seething, Eli grasped every ounce of self-control he could find and kept his hands—and words—to himself. But he'd be doing a little digging. Like finding out this guy's name and anything else that might be important.

It didn't take a genius to realize that Holly might need to be a little more concerned about the strange things happening to her.

Silently he promised to keep tabs on the strangers in town and a protective eye on Holly. Watching the stranger leave, Eli loped back to his car, climbed in and went to find Holly.

Holly thought her brain might rupture through her skull. Never had she been so furious with someone as she was with the man who'd grabbed her.

Or so scared.

When he'd grabbed her arm outside the police station…

Fingers rubbed the bruised area and she vowed to keep her eyes open, including the ones she intended to grow in the back of her head.

Shaking, unsure of the right thing to do, she stared at the wall. The man's words rang in her ears. "I have a message for you, Holly. Good offers only come along every so often. Wise up and take advantage of the chance to sell your land before someone gets hurt. You never know who might be a victim, especially little old ladies recovering from cancer. Tell anyone about my visit and you'll regret it."

After a quick call to her mother to reassure herself that the woman was fine, she bit her lip and pondered her options. Go to Alex and report the assault? It was her word against the man's and she didn't even know who he was. She couldn't ever remember seeing him around before.

God? What's going on? Why does someone want my property so badly? Sure, it's worth money, but not that much, is it?

Popping two ibuprofen tablets chased with a swallow of water, she read the document spread out on her desk. Jessica manned the front counter while Holly worked to get herself under control.

Transcross Realty had gone too far this time. Threatening her and her mother was more than just simple harassment. But what should she do? Go to Alex? After their confrontation just a little while ago, she dreaded the thought, but knew she might have to break down and do it.

Transcross had upped their offer another five thousand dollars. She picked up the phone and dialed the number listed at the top of the paper.

"This is Patrick Zimmerman."

"Mr. Zimmerman, this is Holly Maddox. I've got in front of me…"

"Oh, yes, Ms. Maddox. You're the young lady with the mountain property I'm trying to talk you into selling."

"That would be me."

"So, have you called to tell me that I'm being more than generous?"

"No, actually, I'm calling to tell you to stop harassing me about this. Tell your goons I'm not selling my home, my land or anything at any price. You need to tell them I don't scare easily and to keep their hands off me or I'll be pressing charges."

"What are you talking about? I don't have any goons and I certainly wouldn't try to scare you into selling. But everything has a price." A heavy sigh. "Tell me what it would take to get you to sell. Name your price."

Through gritted teeth, she said, "It's not for sale."

With controlled movements, almost as though moving in slow motion, she hung up the phone and replaced it on the base.

Then she put her head in her hands and did her best to muffle her frustrated scream.

The door burst in. "Are you okay?"

Jessica.

Holly hadn't been as discreet with the scream as she'd tried to be.

She looked up. "Sorry. I think I just have a little too much stress in my life right now."

"What's going on?" Concern etched her friend's face.

Before she had a chance to answer her friend, Eli spoke from behind Jessica as he slipped past her and into the office. "Who was that guy, Holly? The one outside the police station?"

Jessica's eyes shot wide as they bounced between Holly and him. Agitation oozed from him.

Holly just stared at the tight-lipped man in front of her. His eyes blazed. He must have seen the man outside the sheriff's office. Bent on escaping, she hadn't noticed Eli watching. Irritated that he felt that he had the right to butt into her business—never mind the fact that she'd turned to him for help last night—she clipped, "What?"

"The guy who grabbed you. What did he say?"

At a loss for words, Holly stared at the man in front of her for a full ten seconds before saying, "Don't worry about it. It wasn't anything I can't handle." She hoped.

His eyes narrowed. "You don't want my help?"

"Not this time. No. I had to learn to deal with stuff all on my own when you left me six years ago. I've gotten pretty good at it."

Jessica slipped out the connecting door into the front of the store. Holly wanted to tell her to stay.

Then Eli said, "So why did you call me last night?"

"The lesser of two evils," she shot back.

He took a deep breath and she was willing to bet he bit his tongue in the process. Then he said, "Something's going on with you and I think you're in more danger than you're aware of."

FOUR

She didn't want to hear it. Not from him anyway. A momentary lapse in judgment had had her asking him for help. It wouldn't happen again.

Holly moved to the back shelf and grabbed an inventory form.

"How's your mother?" His question came from left field.

"Hanging in there." She kept her eyes on the form, concentrated on filling in the blanks as she counted items.

"Look, Holly, can we talk for a minute?"

"About what?"

He reached out and took her hand, stilling the pen's movement across the paper.

She pulled away.

Fair enough. "I've missed you."

Now she went rigid. "Eli…"

"No, let me finish."

She snapped her lips together. Lips that used to smile and turn his heart to mush. Lips he used to kiss and trace with his finger. Lips that used to tell him how wonderful he was and how much she loved him.

Oh, boy, had he ever messed up. *God, help me make this right.*

He swallowed. Hard. "I wanted to say I'm sorry, Holly."

She wilted like sails on a windless day. The pen clinked on the floor. "Excuse me?"

"I'm… I said I was sorry."

"For?" Her incredulous, sometimes gray, sometimes blue eyes stared at him.

He cleared his throat. "For treating you the way I did when we were in high school and then after I got home from the academy six years ago."

Lost for words, she just stared at him, inventory sheet forgotten. "Are you dying or something?"

He choked.

This time it was his turn to stare at her. "No, I'm not dying. Why would you ask that?"

"Because this is just so…" She waved a hand as though she thought she could snatch the words she needed from the air around her.

"So…?"

"So not like you, I guess. I don't ever remember you apologizing for anything…ever."

The slap of her words jerked him back. Had he truly been so arrogant and prideful? So full of himself that he never considered her feelings?

Shame filled him. Yes, he had.

This time, it was he who had a hard time meeting her eyes. "I'm truly sorry for that, Holly. I'm a different person today than I was all those years ago."

Skepticism greeted those words and while it grated, he also understood the source of it.

"What changed you?"

"God."

Some of the skepticism faded. Shock, then interest flickered. "Why God now? As I recall, you used to indulge me in going to church with me when we were in high school, but you always said you never put much stock in God or religious things."

"I know. Then I became a cop."

"Seems to me that might convince you more than ever that God didn't have much to do with the world and those in it."

Surprised at her astuteness, he nodded. "At first."

"Then?"

"Then I got a preacher for a partner."

A brow lifted. At least he wasn't boring her.

"He could find God in any situation. Didn't matter if it was a homicide or a burglary. I'll never forget. We had a young mother killed by her husband. We got him and the evidence to convict him. But something about that case really got to me and all of the 'God is still good' stuff my partner kept spouting bugged me. I finally shouted at him, 'Where was God when this guy was beating the life out of her?' He looked like I'd slapped him. Then he said something like, 'Eli, I don't understand evil, I don't understand God's way all the time. What I do know is that at least the children who were supposed to be home, weren't. That was an act of God.' I've never forgotten that."

"Oh."

"A neighbor had come by to take the kids to play at the park. That's why they weren't home."

"Your partner sounds like an exceptional man. Where is he now?"

"With the God he loved so much."

She flinched. "I'm so sorry. Was he killed in the line of duty?"

"No. Cancer."

Tears welled in her eyes. "I'm sorry," she repeated.

His own throat felt too tight so he cleared it, shoved his hands into his pockets and paced the small area between the shelves where she stood and the back door that she now had armed. "I miss him. But his influence…" He shrugged, finding it hard to get the words out. "Watching him die, I was helpless in a way that's hard to describe. I've never lost anyone really close to me. I mean my mom ran off but that was her choice. But losing him…"

Her rapt attention spurred him on.

"Watching Mark go through what he did and his wife standing right by his side through the whole thing…"

"Makes you evaluate your own life, doesn't it?"

She understood. She'd been through it, was going through it, with her mother. Of course she understood.

"Yes, exactly. One day I woke up and realized I wanted that kind of faith…and that kind of woman by my side. And I wanted to be the kind of man Mark was. I know I have a long way to go, but I hope I'm at least making some progress."

Holly set the clipboard with the inventory sheet onto her desk. "I'm glad for you, Eli."

He cocked his head. "Thanks. I think."

Unsure how to respond, she walked to the large refrigerator on the back wall and opened the door. "I have to make a delivery to Sue Anne at the diner."

"What is it?"

"A Valentine's basket." She pulled it from the refrigerator. Full of fresh fruit, chocolate and a teddy bear, it was pretty heavy. With a grunt, she set it on the table and pulled two balloons from the plastic bin to her left.

Helium squealed as it whooshed into the latex. Two ribbons and a pretty bow around the handle of the basket and she was ready. "Sue Anne's husband is in Iraq. He knew she'd be visiting her folks in Virginia for Valentine's and wanted me to deliver it early."

"Nice. I'll go with you."

"It's not necessary."

"I'm not doing it out of necessity. And we have a pickup to make, remember?"

Looking at his stiff jaw and narrowed eyes, she wondered if it would be worth the energy arguing with him.

Deciding it wasn't, she made her way to the front of the store to inform Jessica where she was going.

Two silent minutes later, Eli opened the door to the diner for her.

And she ran smack into Alex.

When he spotted them, he stopped and narrowed his eyes. Eli shifted and prepared for a confrontation. Alex didn't like them being together, that was obvious, but then the man's expression softened, morphed into a sheepish grin. "Holly, Eli."

"Alex," Holly said, wariness oozing from her.

He cleared his throat. "Uh. I just wanted to say I've been working on the break-in at your store and so far I've come up pretty empty, sorry."

Reading Alex wasn't easy. And Eli was pretty good at judging whether or not people were sincere. But Alex stumped him.

But Holly offered the man a smile, saying, "I appreciate you spending so much time on it. Maybe something will turn up."

"Well, you look like you're busy," Alex noted.

Eli watched the man walk to a booth and slide in. "Isn't that Jarrod Parker, your lawyer, with him? I seem to remember him from high school, too."

She looked. "Yeah, Jarrod's married to Alex's sister."

Then her eyes went wide once more and she whispered, "That's him."

"That's who?"

"The guy that…stopped…me outside the sheriff's office. In the booth next to Alex and Jarrod."

Eli tilted his head for a look at the man in khaki slacks, a knit collared shirt and sunglasses. He sat alone in the back booth.

She drew in a breath and grunted. The basket clutched in her left hand seemed to have gained weight since leaving her store. "What is his deal?

"I'll go ask him," Eli said.

"No. Leave it be."

"If he's following you, I want to ask him about it."

"And have him say what?" she protested as she shifted the basket to the other hand. "It's a restaurant, Eli, he'll say he's here to eat. That's not against the law."

"What did he say to you out there on the sidewalk?"

Should she tell him?

The man's threat against her mother rang in her mind. *Tell anyone about our little visit and you'll regret it.*

Eli leaned closer. "What are you not telling me, Holly?"

Gulping, Holly looked back at the man in the booth. His gaze drilled her and she swallowed hard. "Nothing, Eli. Just let me deliver this and I'll be ready to leave."

Eli looked like he wanted to argue with her. Instead, he said nothing as she hid her quaking fear of the man in the booth and walked over to a short, thin woman in her mid-thirties. When Sue Anne saw the basket, she squealed and threw her arms around Holly. "Thank you so much."

"Call your husband and thank him. Happy Valentine's Day."

In a hurry to escape the watchful eyes of the stranger, Holly didn't linger and a minute later, she stepped out of the restaurant and headed for her car. She just wanted to get away, far away from the man and his threats. And she wanted to check on her mother.

Eli followed close behind her.

Ignoring the cold cutting through her down coat, she used a shaking hand to grab her phone.

Good offers only come along every once in a while. Take advantage of it before someone gets hurt.

Clenching her fist around the phone, she considered whether or not to tell Eli about the threat. She wanted to, but what if he confronted the guy and the guy hurt her mother?

He opened the door to her truck as she dialed the number. Sliding in the driver's seat, she cranked it and turned on the heat. Eli climbed in the passenger side just as her mother answered.

"Hi, Mom. Are you doing okay?"

"Fine, darling." Holly heard the tolerant tone in her mother's voice. The woman knew Holly worried and put up with her daughter's frequent calls. "I'm sitting here reading a book. Duster and Sassy are out chasing squirrels and Millie, the pastor's wife, called to say she'd be here in about thirty minutes to visit awhile."

"Oh, good. Well, have a nice visit and I'll give you a call when I'm headed home, all right?"

"Sounds good, dear."

She hung up the phone.

Blowing out a breath, Holly focused on what she needed to get done. She'd think about telling Eli about the threat, but right now, they had a pickup to make. From the corner of her eye, she caught movement.

The man from the booth was standing in the door of the restaurant, watching. She opened her mouth to tell Eli when the stranger lifted a finger to his lips in warning. Holly snapped her lips together and glanced at Eli. He was punching a text message into his phone.

Her eyes shot back to the man.

Still watching, threatening.

Was her mother really in danger? Would the man really do something if he found out she said something? Did she dare take a chance? Could she afford *not* to?

Oh, Lord, tell me what to do.

Shivering, her eyes followed her watcher as he turned back into the restaurant.

After Eli clicked his seat belt into place and dropped his phone into his shirt pocket, she ignored the little inner voice urging her to share her fears and asked him, "Are you ready to get your ear talked off?"

No, she wouldn't tell him anything. Elva Sharp had thrown them together for this afternoon. But in a couple of hours, they would go their separate ways and she wouldn't have anything more to do with Eli and his heartbreaking actions.

Eli raised a brow. "What do you mean?"

She kept her voice neutral, polite. "Mrs. Sharp. She's a widow who lives alone, but has been so good to Mom. She's always bringing over food or just stopping by to talk."

"Ah, yes. She taught me Sunday school about a hundred years ago. I hadn't realized Mr. Sharp had died."

"About a year ago. I try to go see her every couple of weeks or so. She's got a real sweet tooth so I take a box of chocolates with me when I go." She held up the box she'd snitched from the store yesterday and couldn't help the smile that tilted her lips. "Don't worry, she'll share." His soft look made her heart stutter. "What?"

"You really have the proverbial heart of gold, don't you?"

Embarrassed at that pronouncement, she gave a halting chuckle and a small smile. "Well, I don't know about that, I just know I like the woman and enjoy doing something nice for her."

A glance in the mirror showed an empty road behind her. No one followed. Relaxing a little, she wasn't prepared for his next question.

"I really messed up, didn't I?"

He was serious. Her smile faded and she shot him a grim look. "I sure thought so at the time." Then she shrugged and sighed. "But who knows, Eli? Maybe you had to travel the path you took in order for you to find God. Or at least be willing to meet Him when you noticed Him."

He blinked. Then turned to watch the passing scenery. Quiet echoed in the truck cab, then he pulled in a deep breath. "I never thought of that."

She smiled, compassion—and maybe a little bit of leftover love?—tugged at her. Oh, no, did she want to go down that road? Her heart mocked her. *You still have feelings for him,* it insisted. With a sinking swoop in her stomach, she realized she did. She could easily allow herself to fall for him again. Zipping her lips into a straight line, she vowed to say nothing else on a personal level.

His quiet sigh told her that he sensed her withdrawal.

Holly pulled into Mrs. Sharp's driveway. The smooth concrete felt good under the tires and she vowed to call someone soon to come out to her home and pave the drive. She almost had enough saved. Maybe next month.

Mrs. Sharp met them at the door of her small well-tended mountain bungalow. A whiff of apple pie followed her out the door. Holly knew what she'd be having for dessert tonight. She looked at the man next to her wishing she dared offer to share. Oh, how she'd missed him.

But her brain sounded alarm signals to her heart.

You don't know that he's here to stay. You've already let him burn you twice, you won't survive a third time.

Taking heed of her internal warning, she placed a smile on her lips and greeted the small woman with a gentle hug. The scent of apple pie, cinnamon and mothballs greeted her. Holly pulled in a long breath and said, "We made it."

"Well, come along. My granddaughter came to visit last month and she helped me do some serious cleaning. I can't believe all the stuff I had tucked away. My goodness, the things a body doesn't need and can live without, why…"

She went on and Holly couldn't help the amusement she knew she had stamped on her face. Eli shot her a grin, her heart did that flip-flop thing, and together they went about loading Holly's truck. The hard work kept them warm in the frigid air.

An hour later, armed with antiques and to-go cups of sweet tea, she and Eli climbed back into the truck.

"Go to the waterfall," he said suddenly.

"What?" She just looked at him.

"I want to go see the waterfall."

"Why?"

Frustration flashed briefly. "Just humor me, will you?"

After a moment, she nodded. "Sure, okay." She put the truck in gear and took the long way, wondering why he wanted to go to the waterfall.

Their waterfall.

The place where they'd shared their first kiss. Her heart thudded, and her lips actually tingled at the memory.

"Do you remember bringing me up here?" he murmured.

Cheeks flushed, embarrassment rolled over her. How immature she must have seemed to him. "I remember."

She wanted to roll down the window of the truck and let the cold mountain air blow in. But then she'd have to explain why she was so warm.

"I've thought a lot about those days with you, Holly."

"Hmm." *Then why did you leave me?* she wanted to shout at him. Instead, she bit her tongue and refused to let the words cross her lips.

Picking up on her signals, he didn't say another word until they'd reached the small clearing beside the waterfall where she parked.

Climbing out of the truck, she let the sound of the falls rush over her. So peaceful up here.

And cold. She shivered. A faint sound reached her ears. "Do you hear that?"

Cocking his head, he listened. "No, just the sound of the waterfall. Why?"

"I thought I heard a motor or something."

Another minute passed as he listened. "No, I don't hear anything."

"All that shooting up in the big city damaged your hearing, huh?" She couldn't help the dig even as uneasiness quivered through her. She wondered why.

Looking around, she couldn't have asked for a more peaceful scene.

Eli slanted her a look. "Cute." He looked at his phone. "I was going to check on Dad, but I've got no signal up here. Battery's getting low, too."

She grunted. "No, no cell towers out here. It's funny because my house isn't too far from here. About a mile and a half that way and I get cell service. Up here, we're back in the dark ages." She squinted through the bare trees. "See that little dot through there?"

"Yeah."

"It's a small log cabin. It belongs to Alex. This time of year you can stand in his yard and look down on mine. He said he wanted to build the cabin up and add on to it for the big

amily he plans to have." She shook her head in disgust. "If
e ever moves up here, I'm going to have to sell my land just
o get away from him."

"We'll figure something out before it comes to that, I
romise." He took her hand and her first instinct was to pull
way. *Don't get too close,* her head warned her. But the feel
f his fingers wrapped around hers broke down a barrier and
he let him pull her along. "Come on, let's go down."

She followed, trying not to tremble at the feel of her hand
n his. "Thank you for helping me today."

"You're welcome."

She shot him a tender look. "How is your dad doing?"

"A little sore after his appointment this morning, but
Buckeye gave him a pain pill so he should be relatively com-
ortable in a little while."

"It's good of you to come home and take care of him. How
ong are you staying?"

They climbed down in silence for a few minutes. Then he
aid over the roar of the falls, "I'm home for good, Holly."

He looked like he was serious. But he'd been serious the
ast time he'd said that, too. He'd come home from the
cademy, accepted a position with the local sheriff's depart-
nent, then six months later resigned and moved to New York.

She kept her mouth shut.

He jumped to the bottom next to the water. Spray misted
hem and she decided they were crazy for doing this in the
niddle of February. He shouted over the rushing water. "I
on't blame you for your skepticism, but I'm serious. I've
nissed this place no matter how hard I've tried to deny it. And
Dad needs me on the farm right now."

"What are you going to do when he doesn't need you
nymore?" she shouted back.

He flinched. "That's the question that keeps me awake at
ight. I guess God's going to have to let me know what He
vants me to do in that regard."

God. She blinked at his easy reference—and the reverence

in his tone. Six years and already his faith was strong maturing at a speed she never would have believed if she hadn't seen it for herself.

"And if He wants you to return to New York?"

He just looked at her. "Then I'd have to go."

"You really have changed, haven't you?"

"Yes."

Could it be that easy? She so wanted to believe he'd changed, but wasn't ready to put her heart on the line only to find out different.

"Hmm."

Pebbles and dirt rained down on them, rolling from the top from where they'd climbed down. Shrieking, Holly jumped to the side to get out of the way.

Eli looked up. "Wonder where that came from?"

Uneasiness shivered through her. "I don't know. That's weird. You think someone else is up there?" Still getting misted from the spray, the cold seeped in through her heavy down coat. "I'm freezing, Eli, let's go."

But he simply grinned at her. "I have very fond memories of this place."

This time the shiver had nothing at all to do with the cold. It was pure Eli. And the memory of their first kiss.

More dirt and rocks rolled down, this time pinging off her face. She brushed the stinging particles away and moved closer to the water. Eli frowned and grabbed her hand and looked up as though he expected to see something. "Come on, I don't like this. We're taking the long way back up."

Her hand snug in his, she followed him as he took a zigzag path up through the trees. Heart pounding, she wondered what might meet them at the top of the falls. By the time Eli pulled her the rest of the way up, her breath came in pants and her leg muscles ached.

Eyes darting, expecting something to jump out at them from behind every tree, she scurried behind Eli. "Do you see anything?"

"No."

"Hear anything?"

"Just the waterfa— Wait a minute. What's that?" A low hum, then a roar met her ears.

"I don't like this, Eli, let's get out of here."

Approaching the truck, she saw the flash of Eli's weapon tucked under his arm in a shoulder holster. It made her feel a little safer.

She reached the truck and stopped. "Eli?"

"Yeah?" His gaze was still focused on the woods in the direction the noise had come from. Now all was silent except for the rush of the water.

"Eli. Come here."

Turning, he made his way over to the truck. "What is—" He broke off as he saw what had her attention. "Well, well, looks like Alex has struck again."

A dozen red roses lay scattered across the hood of Holly's truck.

FIVE

Arriving at the church, Holly breathed a sigh of relief. The roses had bothered her. Not the flowers themselves, but the fact that Alex had followed her up to the falls and left them for her, especially since he knew she was traveling with Eli. Why did he continue to try so hard? Why would he continue to want to be with someone who didn't return his affection?

Doing her best to push Alex to the back of her mind, she found four other workers already there sorting through the collected items. Hiram Fellows and Pete Owens met them at the entrance to the gym. While the guys unloaded, Holly made her way inside to greet the other two ladies on the committee with her. Hiram's and Pete's wives.

"Holly, welcome to the madhouse," Mary Fellows offered with a chuckle. She had her long gray hair pulled up into a smooth ponytail. Janine Owens, forty years younger and a newlywed, flashed her bright smile and said, "We wondered when you were going to show up. Alex is inside." She winked and nudged Holly with an elbow.

Dread evaporated the happy face she'd pasted on. Giving a weak smile, she said, "It took me a little longer than I thought it would."

Alex came out of the building dressed in jeans and a heavy down overcoat. "Hey there, darlin'."

"I'm not your darlin'," she muttered under her breath. Obviously returning his gifts had accomplished nothing. Anger stirred. "Did you leave roses on my truck a little while ago?"

Innocence radiated from him. *"Moi?"*

Fake innocence. Holly snapped her mouth shut. He simply looked pleased with himself. Then he took her hand and pulled her to the side. "Come on, Holly, give me another chance. I promise if you just spend some more time with me, you'll see I'm a good guy."

Hating the hurt she saw on his face, remembering her own shattered heart when Eli had left her, she tried to soften the blow once again. "Don't do this, Alex."

Pleading puppy-dog eyes stared back at her. She refused to let that affect her. "Now leave me alone…*please.*"

Dropping his hand, she brushed past him. Feeling eyes on her, she saw Eli watching with narrowed eyes. However, if he had anything to say, he kept it to himself.

"Hey, Holly!"

She turned. Mary waved her over to the table where she was working, putting prices on various items. "Do you mind seeing if you can find some more price tags for me? I think there's some in the workroom, in the file cabinet next to the closet."

"Sure, I'll be happy to."

Holly watched from the door for a moment as Eli and Alex worked to unload the recliner from her truck which Mrs. Sharp donated. Eli's long-sleeved T-shirt clung tightly to him. His heavy coat lay tossed to the side and hung over the edge of the truck bed.

"Holly? The tags?"

Jerked from her admiring stupor, she blushed and hurried toward the workroom. Berating herself for acting like she was back in high school mooning over some guy, she made her way down the darkened corridor then turned left.

In the workroom, she flipped on the light and went to the file cabinet.

Just as she opened the drawer, the lights went off. For a

moment, she didn't move, just froze. Thoughts of the break-in at the store, the scare at her house, the waterfall, Alex's gifts, the roses, the…noise in the hallway.

Darting to the door, she looked out. Just a dark hall, no light coming from anywhere. "Eli? Alex? Mary?"

No answer. Shaking her head at her paranoia, she turned back to see if she could feel her way around the desk. Surely there would be a flashlight somewhere.

A scrape.

She darted back to the door and peered out again.

Heavy breathing. More footsteps. A door closing?

A flashlight beam rounded the corner.

She opened her mouth to call out again then snapped it shut. What if it wasn't someone she wanted to meet in a dark hallway? What if it was the person who was outside her home last night? What if…

She stepped back and shut the door with a quiet click and twisted the lock.

Heart hammering in her throat, she reached for her cell phone.

The doorknob rattled….

"Hey, Holly? You in here?"

Relief washed through her. Eli.

Opening the door, she rushed out. The flashlight beamed across her face. Eli gripped her upper arms. "Are you all right?"

"I'm fine. A little scared, but fine. What happened to the lights?"

"I think we blew a fuse or something. I was looking for the breaker box. Mary said it was back here. She said you were, too, and for me to keep an eye out for you."

"Why didn't you answer when I called out?"

His forehead crinkled. "I didn't hear you call out."

It was her turn to frown. She'd heard footsteps and heavy breathing. He should have been close enough to hear her. "Oh. Okay."

So, it hadn't been him in the hall?

"Come on," he encouraged. "I'll help you find the tags. And by the way, Alex left. Said he got a call he had to take care of."

Gladness filled her. Good, she could finish what she needed to do without stumbling over Alex every few steps.

Two minutes later, Eli had the breaker switch thrown and the lights came back on.

She looked at him. "Thanks."

He grinned that grin that made the hairs on the back of her neck stand up and the butterflies in her stomach start to dance.

Before she could do something stupid like throw herself into his arms and make him promise he was really back to stay, she turned and headed back to the gym.

Eli brought up the rear.

Soon, everything was in order. Items separated, classified and tagged. The work completed for now, Holly said she'd lock up. The two couples said their goodbyes and left, leaving Holly and Eli alone in the church.

"Whew." Holly sat on the bottom bleacher and wiped a hand across her forehead. "That's hard work."

Eli nodded and joined her as he drained the last of Mrs. Sharp's to-go cup of tea. "I admire what you all are doing here."

"Thanks." Holly had finished her tea an hour ago. She licked her lips and vowed to bring a stash of water with her next time. "It's worth it to keep the orphanage up and running. I've only made one visit, but I plan to go again in the summer."

"How do you go and not come home with a couple of children?"

Bowing her head, she stared at the floor then said quietly, "It's not easy, that's for sure. Maybe if I was married…" She shrugged, not needing to go there. Not with Eli.

"Eli? You in here?"

"Buckeye?" Eli jumped up, worry paling his face. "What is it? What's wrong?"

"It's your daddy, he's taken a fall. I called the ambulance to come get him. They're taking him into Bryson City to the hospital. I sure hope he didn't reinjure that leg of his."

"What? Why didn't you call?"

"I did. It went straight to voice mail. I knew you were going over to Elva's so called her and she said you'd probably be here."

Eli pulled out his cell phone and groaned. "Dead battery."

Holly rose and joined them. "Go be with your dad, Eli. I'll just lock up here and be on my way."

He hesitated. "Lock up and let me see you get safely in your truck."

"All right, I'll hurry."

Three minutes later, she was in her truck watching Buckeye's taillights disappear down the road.

Lord, please let Eli's father be all right. I know how worried he is right now. Fill him with Your peace and love.

She placed the key in the ignition and turned it.

Nothing happened.

What?

She tried again.

Not even a sputter.

A flame of fear ignited in the pit of her belly.

Just ahead of her two headlights suddenly pierced the darkness and a motor gunned.

The flame of fear became an inferno.

SIX

Adrenaline pumping, Holly scrambled for her cell phone. The headlights crept closer.

What to do?

Sit there like a paper target?

Run back into the church? Would she have time to unlock the door, get in and get it closed before he could grab her?

With shaking fingers, she punched in 9-1-1.

"What's your emergency?"

"I... I'm... I..." What did she say? What *was* her emergency? "My truck won't start. I'm stuck at the Community Church on Rosewood Drive."

"Holly?"

"Trish?"

"Yeah, what's wrong? You sound terrified."

"I am."

The headlights flickered off. No one made any move to exit the car. Thanks to the lone parking lamp stationed to the rear of the vehicle, she could make out the head and shoulders of a figure sitting behind the wheel.

"Sit tight. I'll have Alex come out and give you a hand."

Of course. Alex. If she hadn't been so scared, she would have laughed. Even the dispatcher, a friend who attended the same church as Holly, knew about her and Alex. "There's a car parked in front of me. He turned his headlights on as I got in my truck. Now they're off and he's just sitting there. Stay on the phone with me, okay?"

"Holly, I'm unable to locate Alex at the moment. I'm dispatching a car, all right? I'll be glad to stay on the phone."

Holly watched the figure move; the head looked left, then right. What was he doing?

Making sure he didn't have any witnesses to the crime he was about to commit? *Lord, what do I do? Why didn't I ask Eli to wait until I could follow behind him?*

Because he was scared about his father and she'd pushed him to hurry.

The figure bent over. She couldn't make out the features. Who was it? The man who'd grabbed her outside the sheriff's office? The person who'd tried to break in her house? Why didn't he get out of the car?

"Holly, are you still there?" Trish asked.

"I'm here."

"What about the car with the headlights? Is it still there?"

"Yes." She could hear herself panting, the fear making her short of breath. Adrenaline made her hands spasm. "The guy's just sitting there. This is really creeping me out, Trish."

"I agree. It's kind of weird. Just stay put. Joel's patrolling over near the church. He's on the way. What is the guy doing?"

"Nothing." The car door opened. A booted foot landed on the gravel beneath the door. "Wait," she squeaked, "he's getting out of his car. Where's Joel?"

"On his way. I told him it was an emergency. Do you have any kind of weapon on you?"

She wanted to cry. "No. Um…wait." Leaning over, she ran her hand under the seat. Fingers closed around the tire iron. "I don't think it'll do much to stop a bullet, though."

"Hold on to it."

Flashing blue lights appeared in the distance, then disappeared as the cruiser rounded a curve. Came back into view.

The person, now in front of his car, paused, focused on the patrol car heading his way.

Then he whirled, climbed back into the car, gunned the engine and sped away.

Holly blinked. Fear slowly ebbed from her. "Joel is here, Trish. Thanks for your help."

"No problem." Trish hung up.

By the time Joel pulled into the parking lot, Holly had the trembling somewhat under control.

She hopped out of her truck and met him as he spun up next to her and lowered his window. Before he could speak, she asked, "Did you see a car on your way up here?"

"Yeah. Why?"

"Because that's the guy that was sitting here scaring me."

"Stay here, I'm going after him."

He wheeled the cruiser and shot after the man who'd scared her. Not taking any chances on the fact that he might double back, she opened the church, walked in and locked the door behind her.

Then she took watch from the window.

Ten minutes later, headlights once again approached and she tensed, ready to run and find a hiding place. The car passed under the outside light and she realized it was Joel.

Stepping back outside, she waited for him to pull up beside her and roll his window down. He propped an arm on the door. "I didn't see anyone. Sorry."

A siren sounded in the distance and Joel got on his radio. After some crackling communication, he turned to her. "That was Alex, he heard what was going on and is headed up here."

Holly sighed. "Okay, can you figure out what's wrong with my truck?" She just really wanted to leave.

"Sure." Joel climbed from his cruiser, flashlight in hand.

Holly popped the hood and he began his investigation. As he worked, she leaned against the front grille beside him. He cleared his throat. "So, what's the deal with you and Alex?"

"There is no more deal."

"Huh."

"What does that mean?"

"Means he's still got his eye on you."

Perturbed, she looked at him but he still had his head buried under the hood. "Why do you say that?"

"Because he's always talking about you."

"Joel…"

"Seriously. He even talks about the kids you guys are going to have."

Not good. "Joel, look at me." He did. "I'm not going to marry Alex, all right? We dated, found out we're completely incompatible, and have gone our separate ways. Understand?"

Narrowed eyes stared at her from under wild brows. "Sure, if you say so."

"I say so."

"I don't think Alex gets that, though. He asked me just the other day if I thought you were a diamond or a pearl type. Here's your problem." He pointed to a cable. "Your battery's disconnected. Probably shook loose."

Another patrol car pulled in beside them and Alex got out. "Trouble, Holly?"

Aggravated at his presence, she snapped. "Yes."

He lifted a brow but didn't comment on her surliness. Instead, he looked over Joel's shoulder.

Regret filled her. Smoothing her tone, she said, "I just had that battery put in. It didn't just shake loose." While she'd been in the church, someone had been busy working on her battery. The man from the restaurant? The one who'd been hanging around her shop before bashing her in the head with the trash can?

Breathing deeply, she watched Joel hook the cable back up to the battery. "Thanks, Joel, I appreciate you doing this."

"Anytime, Holly. Want me to follow you home?"

"I'll do it." Alex motioned her to her truck.

"No…um…" She looked around. What if the person who'd been here earlier was just waiting for her to leave the church so he could resume his scare tactics? "Well, maybe. If you're sure it won't be any trouble."

"No trouble at all." Alex opened the door to the truck and

gave her a smile. "It's never any trouble spending time with you, Holly."

Ignoring the intimate undertone, just plain not in the mood to deal with him, she hopped back into her truck. The engine turned over smooth as silk.

Cable came loose, my eye, she thought.

She had to admit she was grateful for the escort home. She just hoped no one lurked outside her house tonight. Eli was in Bryson City with his father. It was up to her to take care of things tonight.

She dialed her mother's number.

"Hi, Mom."

"Oh, Holly. I was just going to call you. Elva asked me if I'd like to go up to that little bed-and-breakfast in Valle Crucis. I told her I'd ride with her."

"Do you feel up to that?"

A pause. "Yes. I'm going to try it, anyway. Today was a pretty good day."

"And you're leaving now? But it's after dark."

"Elva's daughter is going to drive us."

"Oh, okay. When will you be back?"

"Sometime tomorrow evening."

After wishing them a safe trip, she hung up. Actually, her mother getting away might be a good idea. Holly didn't know exactly how much danger she was really in, but she would be able to concentrate on figuring it out a lot better if she didn't have to worry about her mother for a few hours.

But she really didn't want to go home to an empty house. Alone.

In the dark.

Glancing in the rearview mirror, she could see Alex's headlights—and wished they belonged to Eli.

And she was mad at herself for wishing it.

Eli looked up to see Holly walking toward him in the hospital waiting room. He blinked, sure she was a mirage his exhausted brain had dredged up just to play a mean trick on him.

She was still there.

He stood. "Holly?"

"Hi, Eli. I came to keep you company. Do you know anything yet?"

"Dad's with the orthopedic surgeon. They had to take more X-rays so I'm just waiting for them to get back. What are you doing here?"

A tiny lift of her shoulders. "I didn't feel like going home. I was driving around thinking and thought I'd come see if there was anything I could do."

Shrewd eyes studied her. "What happened?"

"What do you mean?"

"Come on, Holly, I was a cop for a lot of years. I can read body language and smell fear a mile away. You're scared." He reached out and grasped one of her hands. Fine tremors still shook it. "See?"

She slumped into one of the plastic seats. "Like I said, I didn't want to go home. My mother decided to go on a little trip and I was afraid…"

"Afraid of what?"

She looked up at him from the corner of her eye. "My truck wouldn't start after you left."

He frowned. "What? It was running fine just a couple of hours earlier. There was never any indication something was wrong."

"That's because I don't think anything was."

She explained the incidents with the headlights and Joel finally arriving to find the disconnected battery cable.

With each word she uttered, Eli felt his blood pressure rise. And the guilt for leaving her behind. He should have made sure she was on her way before taking off. But he'd been so worried about his dad that he'd messed up.

And possibly put Holly in danger because of it. "I'm so sorry, Holly."

She waved a hand. "Don't worry about it. It's not your fault."

Eli placed his hands on her shoulder and when she didn't resist, pulled her close for a gentle hug. His heart thudded at her familiar scent, the coming-home feel of her in his arms. He kissed the top of her head and asked, "Did you see anything at all?"

Without looking up, she said, "I saw somebody. An outline behind the wheel of a car. He positioned himself in a way that kept me from identifying him." She looped her arms around his waist and sighed.

As right and wonderful as it felt to hold her again, his detective instincts kicked into high gear. "What about the car? Did you recognize it?"

Pulling away, she looked up at him and shook her head. "No, but I didn't get a good look at it, either. The lights were too bright and when he left, he was in the dark, so I still couldn't see anything."

"Sir?"

They looked up. Eli squeezed Holly's fingers before letting go and reaching to shake the doctor's hand. Her name tag read Dr. Mary Beth Hill. "Your father's doing fine. We've got him on some pretty strong painkillers so he's out of it right now, but the X-rays show he didn't do any more damage to the broken bone. He's very lucky."

Relief swept over Eli. "Thank you. When can I take him home?"

"I would say tomorrow. We're just going to keep him for observation tonight to make sure we haven't missed anything. If he's still doing well by lunchtime tomorrow, we'll discharge him."

"Great. Thank you so much."

"No problem."

Dr. Hill left and Eli turned to Holly. "Guess I'll be spending the night here tonight."

She nodded and rose. "Then I'll see you later."

"Go on home, boy." Eli turned to see Buckeye standing in the doorway. "We got those people coming to look at the horses in the morning. Since your daddy is laid up here, it's going to be up to you to make the sale. My sister lives just up the road a piece. I'll stay with her tonight and get your dad home tomorrow whenever they spring him."

"But, Buckeye…" Torn, Eli offered a halfhearted protest. He didn't want to leave his dad, but he knew they needed the sale. Buckeye didn't like to handle that end of things and Eli didn't want to ask him to. "All right. Thanks." He looked at Holly. "Want me to follow you home?"

Relief at his offer coated her pretty, fragile face. "Sure, if you don't mind."

"It's kind of on the way." He smiled at her and she reciprocated. His stomach did that funny swooping thing it always did when she looked at him like that. When she let the past go and forgot he'd once acted like a jerk. He really *was* home to stay this time, no matter what she thought. The promotion he'd applied for last month tickled the back of his mind.

Although, if he hadn't heard anything by now, it was probably a sure bet he wasn't going to be offered the job.

But what if you are? What will you do then?

He didn't have an answer for himself.

Pushing those thoughts aside, he motioned for her to go ahead of him, waving goodbye to Buckeye on the way out.

Eli walked her to her car. "I'm parked around the other side. Give me a ride to the other parking lot and I'll follow you home."

"Okay. I'm glad your dad didn't hurt himself any worse."

"I know." He shook his head. "He's so stubborn. Won't listen to a word I tell him."

"Hmm. Sounds like someone else I know."

He shot her a look, guilt pinging him once again. She was right. Ten years ago, even six years ago, he'd known everything. "I'm not like that anymore."

She cocked an eyebrow at him. "If you say so."

He got out when she parked next to his car then turned to peer back in at her. "I'm going to prove it to you."

"How?"

He just looked at her. "I have no idea, but I hope you'll give me the chance to work on it."

Eli climbed into his car, mind and heart churning. More than ever he wanted to be back in Holly's good graces. He couldn't bear the thought of her pushing him away forever. Even if she decided she couldn't ever trust him with her heart again and he had to settle for just friendship, he'd start there.

He wondered if Alex felt the same way. Part of Eli sympathized with the man if that was the case, but the other part of him vowed to keep Holly away from him.

No matter what the cost.

SEVEN

The Transcross Realty vehicle parked in her driveway made Holly gape in disbelief. "You've got to be kidding me," she muttered as she yanked on her clothes.

A glance at the clock made her blink again. Seven-twelve. The sun had barely put in an appearance this morning when she'd heard someone crunching the gravel on her driveway. Thinking about how wonderful it had been to be held by Eli once again had kept her awake into the wee hours of the morning. Now this.

Bolting down the steps, she stopped at the front door and gathered her composure—and her temper. As an afterthought she snatched her cell phone from the table beside the door.

With an outward calm that hid the boiling anger inside her, she stepped outside to find two men, their backs facing her, taking pictures of her property. "Excuse me, may I help you gentlemen with something?"

They whirled. "Um, good morning, miss." The one with the thick glasses held out a hand then dropped it when she crossed her arms. "I'm Preston Hancock and this is my associate, James Miller. We're from Transcross Realty."

"I got that much." She gestured to the car. "What I don't understand is why you're in my front yard."

"Our boss, Mr. Zimmerman, sent us out here to take pictures. Said you were selling."

A frustrated yell wanted to rupture from her throat. She swallowed, stepped forward and planted her hands on her hips. He backpedaled two steps. James Miller's face remained impassive. "Let's get one thing straight right now," she insisted. "I'm not selling. And I'm just past the point of being nice about it."

He blinked owlishly behind his thick glasses. "Excuse me? But…but…"

Patience, Holly. "I've also sent that statement in writing to Mr. Zimmerman. Now get off my property before I call the cops and have you charged with trespassing."

Mr. Miller's jaw went hard. "Lady, Mr. Zimmerman wants this property." Menace dripped from him and for the first time, she noticed his eyes. Hard eyes. Mean eyes.

Fear darted through her as she thought about the man who'd accosted her outside the sheriff's office, but she ignored it. "Please leave and don't come back."

His lip curled. "Better take the man's very generous offer. You never know when you might need the extra money."

"Just what are you threatening me with?" Was this really happening? First the man outside the sheriff's office, then this? And what about last night? What if it was someone from Transcross sent to scare her?

"This is a dangerous area." His hand swept out. "Isolated. Never know when you might end up with a few more medical bills." With that, he gave her one last threatening look then jerked his head toward his partner. "Come on."

Once they were gone, Holly let out a frustrated "Oh!"

Then the uneasy feeling that she was still being watched kicked in. Spinning around, she scanned the surrounding property. Nothing moved or seemed out of place.

Then again, why hadn't the dogs barked when the Transcross guys drove up?

"Duster? Sassy?" She'd let them in the house when she'd gotten home last night, wanting the company. Without her mother there, the house felt empty, lonely.

And somehow threatening.

"Duster? Here boy! Sassy?"

No dogs.

Now her stomach clenched. *Oh, Lord, please don't let anything have happened to them.*

She went back inside and checked the kitchen. They had a doggie door and could come and go as they pleased from the sunporch side of the house.

Holly checked the area but there wasn't any way to tell if the dogs had used the door or not. Since they weren't in the house, she'd have to assume they had.

But where would they go? They never wandered very far. And they'd both greeted her when she'd arrived home last night.

"Duster?" She whistled. "Sassy?"

The faint sound of barking reached her ears.

"Duster?" She closed her eyes, listening.

The shed?

She raced across the back lawn to the utility shed. Pushing the sliding door open, Holly gasped as the two furry animals bolted from the interior. Both immediately went to take care of business, which told her they'd been locked in there for several hours.

But why? Who would do this? Mr. Ryan? But he hadn't even been around for the last few days. And he wouldn't have put the dogs in there anyway.

Between the time she'd gotten home last night to the time she awakened, someone had locked her dogs in the shed.

They bounded up to her, tails pumping ninety miles an hour. She scratched ears while she thought. Then Duster darted into the house via the doggie door while Sassy chased a bird.

Pacing, wondering what this meant and what she should do about it, she eyed the shed. The phone vibrated in her hand and she jumped. She'd forgotten she even had it.

Who would be calling this early? Did she want to answer

it? Not recognizing the number, she paused. Finally, on the last ring, she snapped it to her ear. "Hello?"

"Good morning, Holly."

"Eli? How did you get my number?"

"I'm sorry, is this a bad time? I figured you'd be getting ready for work and wanted to catch you before you left."

Deep breath. "No, no, sorry. Actually, it's been a rather strange morning." She glanced at the clock. An hour had passed since she'd been awakened by the Transcross Vehicle.

"Want to tell me about it at the church? Dad couldn't sleep in spite of his pain meds and kept calling me from the hospital. He decided he had some stuff to get rid of and had me up all night going through it."

"All night?"

"Well, maybe not all night, but I've got quite a load here I need to dump. Want me to pick you up? I've got Miz Hannah's homemade doughnuts."

Ooh, now that was tempting. Her heart hesitated, still not ready to take the risk of spending more time with him, and yet... "Sure, Mom's on a mini vacation so I just need to get ready. Let me meet you there, though, because I'll need my car when we're finished. I've got to run go to the store to open up. Jessica can take care of the store while we're at the church. I also need to finish…um…taking care of some things around here."

His voice sharpened. "What kinds of things?" He must have picked up on the lingering fear in her voice.

She paused then said, "I'll tell you when I see you. Give me a few minutes or so to get everything together and I'll meet you."

He let her get away with the delay. "All right. My buyer called this morning to say he'd be running late so I've got some time to take this stuff to the church before I have to get back here and meet him."

"And you thought I'd help, huh?"

"I knew I could count on you."

She couldn't help the warmth that danced through her, but

listened to the word of caution her brain sent to her heart. His next words made her grimace. "Besides, you're the closest person with a key to the church."

She snorted. "Thanks, Brodie."

Laughter greeted her, then his husky voice lowered. "You know I want to see you, Holly."

She shivered and said, "I'll see you in about an hour."

Hanging up the phone, she groaned. What was she *doing?* Why was she spending time with the man who'd dumped her, not once, but twice? Was she out of her mind?

But he'd changed.

Right, she argued with herself. Did she really want to take a chance on that? Risk having him splatter her heart all over the ground once more?

Part of her did. Part of her desperately wanted to believe it. The more cynical side of her flashed warning signs shouting that she needed more proof than the apology he'd offered the other day. And the fact that he'd put his personal life aside to come take care of his father and run the horse ranch.

As she thought about Eli, she knew for certain why she and Alex didn't work. No one pulled at her like Eli Brodie. She couldn't get the man out of her head—or her heart.

Even though an examination of the shed showed nothing amiss, she was still bothered. If the doors hadn't been the sliding kind that had to have human help to close, she might be tempted to think the dogs had gotten trapped on their own.

But it just wasn't possible.

Someone had shut them in there.

Still pondering, she headed back inside to finish her morning routine.

And then she'd meet Eli at the church. The one man she should probably avoid if she wanted to keep her heart from splintering in two again.

Eli slapped the aftershave on his cheeks and stared at himself in the mirror. Excitement over the upcoming meeting with Holly made him smile. Nervousness made his insides jumpy.

Lord, I know I don't deserve her. In fact if I were her, I'd probably take off running in the opposite direction and not stop until I was covered in her dust. But I'd really like one more chance. You and I both know I'm a different man than I was before. Holly and I had something special and I messed it up. But this time, with You in the mix, I think we could get it right.

Grabbing his coat from the back of the chair where he'd tossed it last night, he slipped it on, snatched up the keys and headed for his truck.

At the end of his driveway, he took a left and climbed the curving road to the next turnoff. Twenty yards later, he spun into the parking lot.

Holly's little red truck sat in front of the church.

Just as he climbed out, she came out of the front door of the church and down the steps toward him. She raised a brow in the direction of his vehicle. "That's quite a load."

At the sight of her, Eli's heart thumped a little faster, sweat slicked his palms. She had on denim jeans, her heavy coat, hat and scarf. She looked adorable.

She reached his truck and he leaned over to hug her. At first, she went stiff, then relaxed. He relished the feel of her in his arms. "Thanks for coming to the hospital last night. It was really good to see you. I needed that."

She placed a hand on his cheek, opened her mouth to say something then snapped it shut when a sheriff's cruiser pulled into the parking lot.

Alex.

Eli heard her indrawn breath as she pulled away. She muttered, "If I didn't know better, I'd swear that man planted a tracking device on me."

Eli felt his ire rise. If Alex didn't back off, he was going to have to have words with him.

Alex climbed from the cruiser.

"What are you doing here?" Holly crossed her arms and leaned back against the truck.

Even though he'd seen the cozy embrace, Alex said nothing. "I got a call about a silent alarm going off." He nodded to the church.

"What?" She straightened. Instant red suffused her face and she darted back to the building. Thirty seconds later, she reappeared. "Is it off now?"

Alex got on the radio, said something, listened, then nodded. "All taken care of."

Holly shook her head. "I'm so sorry."

"No problem." He smiled then looked at Eli's loaded truck. "You need some help?"

Surprised at the offer, Eli studied the man then shrugged. "Sure, since you're here."

Thirty minutes later, Eli's truck bed was empty. Eli rolled his shoulders and decided he liked working as a team with Holly even with the addition of Alex and his determination to compete for Holly's affection. Her fluid grace made every movement a pleasure to watch.

Alex's radio crackled and he stepped away from them for a moment.

Holly locked up the church and Eli pulled his keys from his pocket. "We never did get around to eating those doughnuts."

"Guess I'll have to take a rain—"

"Holly?"

Eli looked up to see Alex coming toward them wearing a frown. Foreboding hit Eli. "What is it?"

Alex looked at Holly. "Someone spray painted graffiti all over your store. The alarm never went off so I don't know if they attempted to get inside, but we need to go take a look."

"What?" Holly didn't wait for an answer. She spun on her heel to head for her truck.

Eli grabbed her arm. "Hold on, Holly, I'll go with you."

Alex intervened. "You're not a cop here anymore, Brodie, remember?"

"I don't care, I'm a friend." He shot a hard look at Alex. The man stared back, some emotion Eli couldn't identify glittering in his dark eyes. Jealousy? Possessiveness?

Finally Alex shrugged. "Fine. Anne, one of the cashiers at the grocery store next door to your store, called it in and Alice radioed me."

The three of them climbed into their respective vehicles and headed down the mountain.

Five minutes later, she pulled up in front of her store, shock pounding through her.

Climbing out of the car, she just stared at the building. Bright red words glared at her. "Time's up," she read in a whisper. She wouldn't say the other painted words out loud, but they burned in her brain nonetheless.

"Who is doing this?" Eli wondered aloud.

"And why?" Alex added.

Anger—and more than a touch of fear—made her fingers shake as she pushed the door open. She couldn't hold back her cry of dismay. "It's been destroyed. All my hard work... Everything..." She wanted to puddle into the floor and wail. Instead, she straightened her spine, sucked back the tears and took in the damage.

Alex laid a hand on her shoulder and she felt too shell-shocked to move away. He turned her to him and said, "I promise I'll get this guy for you."

Eli's gaze darted between them and she gave him a tremulous smile. She moved over to the Valentine's display she'd spent hours putting together. Smashed chocolate, stuffing ripped from the cute teddy bears, flowers strewn across the room. Everywhere she looked, destruction greeted her. "I'll have to refund orders. Valentine's Day is the day after tomorrow. I'll never be able to have this cleaned up in time."

"What about insurance?" Eli asked.

She nodded. "I have insurance, but even with it..." She shook her head and swallowed hard. "I may have to close the store." The phone line had been cut, explaining why the alarm hadn't gone off. The trouble light blinked, telling her she needed to investigate.

That was a lot of help after the fact.

Two hours later, she had her police report filed, and Alex had collected all the evidence he could. Eli had gone back to his ranch to sell his horses and Holly had called her insurance company. Now she set the broom aside, slumped into a chair and stared at the destruction.

Despair hit her. "What's going on, God? I don't understand why all this is happening." The whispered words brought a bit of comfort. She didn't know what was going on, but God did. That was the important thing.

She hated to break the news to her mother, but money was going to be tight from here on out. They still had some insurance money left from her dad, but the medical bills from her mother were no small thing.

Sighing, she wondered briefly if she'd have to sell the house now.

The thought struck her hard, ricocheting against every nerve. She sat up slowly, her brain looping over itself as she processed that thought.

Was that what this was all about?

Once the idea took root, it grew. She remembered the menacing James Miller from Transcross and his subtle threats, the man with the dark glasses that seemed to keep turning up and both men telling her that good offers were rare and she should take advantage of their generosity.

Narrowing her eyes, she contemplated that idea. To some it may sound silly, but what other reason could there be? Her property was the only thing of any real value she and her mother had.

But how could she prove it?

And would anyone even believe her if she said anything?

Eli would. Even if no one else in this town would hear it, Eli would.

But the thought of turning to him for more help scared her.

She remembered the hug in the church parking lot. How right it had felt. How wonderful it had been to feel his arms around her once more.

If he had truly changed...

Time would tell.

Eli parked back in front of Holly's shop. He'd sold the three horses and dropped the payment at the bank. A phone call to check on his dad raised his spirits. Buckeye informed Eli that all was fine, they would be home in time for supper and no, Eli didn't need to make the trip to the hospital. Eli promised to meet them at the house.

Unable to get Holly off his mind, he decided to come back and help her clean up and see what she was going to do now.

As he got out of his truck, he noticed a car sitting two doors down past the grocery store. He'd seen the two men sitting in the sedan as he'd passed by but hadn't thought much about it. Now he realized they had a perfect view of Holly's shop.

Strangers? Tourists?

Of course they could be here for the auction.

However, these guys made his cop instincts hum. They hadn't been there when he'd left a few hours ago. What could they be up to now? And why were they just sitting there watching Holly's store?

He shut the door of his truck and debated whether or not to approach them. He could at least get a license number and have a buddy at his old department run it for him. Just to satisfy his curiosity.

Decision made, Eli headed in their direction. Once they realized they were his intended targets, one said something to the other and the car backed up, did a three point turn and sped down the street.

But not before Eli got a plate number.

Suspicious behavior warranted proactive behavior, he always said. Pulling out his cell phone, he punched in a number.

"Hello?"

"Hey Ken, this is Eli. How ya doing?" Ken Larson, a fellow detective in New York, had been one of his best friends on the force.

"Eli? Good to hear from you. What are you up to? When are you planning on coming back here?"

"My dad was hurt in an accident so I've been helping out around the farm. As far as when I'm coming back…well, I don't guess that's going to happen. You know I applied to be considered for the captain's job and haven't heard anything so…I think maybe I'm exactly where I'm supposed to be."

Silence. "Really?"

"Yeah."

"As far as I know, they haven't made an announcement yet on who the new captain is, so you might be getting a call after all."

That rocked Eli back a moment. He'd completely given up on the position. But all he said was, "We'll see, I suppose."

"So why are you calling?"

"I have a favor to ask."

"Shoot."

Eli gave him the plate number and Ken promised to get back to him.

The door to Holly's store opened and she carried a filled-to-the-rim trash bag.

"Hey, you need some help?"

Her head snapped up. "Eli? What are you doing back?"

"Thought I'd offer my cleaning services."

Her eyes warmed and lingered on his, then she blinked and looked away. "Sure, if you've got the time."

Shooting her a wry look, he said, "What else have I got to do? Buckeye is taking care of Dad, I sold the horses and made a few bucks," he said as he shrugged. "Other than that, I'm feeling pretty useless all in all, I guess."

Holly laughed, a sincere chuckle that shot joy through him. "Eli, you are far from useless. You said you sold your horses."

"True."

She paused and an expression crossed her face. One he'd never seen before and didn't know exactly how to identify. "What?"

Opening her mouth, she started to say something, then stopped and shook her head.

He grabbed her arm in a gentle grip. "What? Come on, you can't look like that and not tell me what you were thinking."

She took a deep breath. "I was thinking that you should run for sheriff."

"Huh?"

A shrug. "I know. Dumb idea, wasn't it? Like a former New York detective would be interested in being a sheriff in a small town place like this." She waved a hand. "Never mind. Momentary lapse of sanity."

Turning, she led him back into the store and handed him a broom.

As he swept, her words lingered in his mind. Run for sheriff? Build a life with Holly? Yeah, he thought, smiling, he could see that happening. He turned to leave.

As he did the vision of the two men in the sedan sitting across the street from Holly's place chased away his pleasant musings. Time to figure out who was threatening Holly. If he didn't, she might not have a future to share with him.

EIGHT

Bundled against the wind and cold, but in need of some exercise, Holly stepped onto the front porch and pulled up short. "Alex?"

He sat in his sheriff's car at the top of the horseshoe-shaped drive and shot her a sheepish grin through the open window. "Hi. You caught me."

"Caught you? What are you doing?"

Duster and Sassy danced at her heels. Then Duster nosed her way up to the car. Through the open window, Alex reached down to scratch the canine's ears. "Working up the nerve to ask you to be my Valentine's date."

Dread curled around her. "Alex, we talked about this...."

He held up the hand that had been on Duster's ears. "I know, I know. But—" He turned to the passenger seat, gathered what was there, then opened his door.

She walked toward him, staring at the bundle of roses that lay in the crook of his arm. "I really care a lot about you, Holly." He shifted and sighed. "Here." Before she could blink, he shoved the roses to her arms, and climbed back in the car.

"Alex, no! I don't want these!"

She tried giving them back, but he refused to take them, saying, "I've got to go, just think about it, will you? At least give me equal time."

"Equal time?" Holly tried one more time to push the

flowers through the open window. One of the buds fell off and landed at her feet.

"I know you and Eli used to be a couple and his coming back here has probably played with your emotions."

"Alex, you've got to stop this!"

His radio cut off her protests. "Gotta go. Just think about it."

Before she had a chance to respond, tires spun on her gravel and his taillights blinked as he headed down her drive.

Helpless, she just stood there a moment then spun on her heel. Walking back up to the front porch, she set the flowers on the rocker then went back down the steps.

With Duster and Sassy at her heels, she made her way to the mailbox at the end of her long drive.

While she walked, she thought. About Alex. What was she going to do with him? Why wouldn't he back off? Pushing thoughts of Alex aside, she kicked a stone in frustration and moved on to more pleasant musings.

While keeping a watchful eye on the area around her.

Her mother had gotten in early last night still looking thin and sickly, yet refreshed, with a new sparkle in her eyes. Thankfully, the remainder of the evening had been quiet.

No one lurked outside her home, no middle of the night disturbances and no hang-up phone calls. After cleaning up her store as much as she could, she and Eli had worked at the church until dark, although she had to admit her heart hadn't been in it. Alex had been there, too, but at least he had behaved himself.

Tomorrow night, the auction would get underway. From what Holly could tell, everything was close to being ready. The workers had given a hundred percent and the church gym nearly bulged with all of the items. Advertisements had gone out into neighboring towns and even into some of the larger cities.

People from all around would make their way to the tiny town of Rose Mountain and from seven p.m. to eleven would bid on the various items. They all knew it was for a wonderful cause and were glad to help.

Opening the mailbox, she spotted an envelope with a yellow rose place carefully on top.

Who? Alex again? No…Eli.

Opening the envelope, she whistled for the dogs and started her trek back to the house. "Come on, guys."

The note said, "Will you meet me at The Steak House for a Valentine's evening? Romance and candlelight to be included. But most importantly, friendship. Then I'll escort you to the auction where we can watch the money roll in for the orphanage."

Her heart caught in her throat.

The Steak House, one of the nicer, pricier restaurants in town, only opened for dinner. Valentine's Day. Tomorrow.

She picked up the single rose and sniffed. Eli. She was falling for him again and realized that at some point she'd finally allowed herself to believe him when he said he was home for good this time.

Still a little part nagged at her. A small kernel of doubt kept her slightly on edge. As though she was waiting for the other shoe to drop.

Back at the house, she gathered the flowers from the rocking chair and stepped inside to find her mother sitting in the den. "Hey," she said as she turned to enter the kitchen to search for two vases.

"I got a phone call," her mother called.

Holly froze as the flowers tumbled from her arms to the sink. She darted back to the den. "The one we've been waiting for?"

"Yes."

"And?"

Her mother rose and held out her hands. Tears dripped from her cheeks. "It's gone. They said I beat it again."

Joy exploded inside her. She felt the smile begin to spread. "You did?"

"We did. You, me and God."

"Oh, thank You, Jesus." Holly pulled her mother into a hug. Sobs of thankfulness shook her. Finally both of them started laughing. And laughing.

It felt good. "So, what…"

The sound of a gunshot, the yelping cry of a wounded animal and the roar of a motorcycle interrupted her words and blended into one roaring sound of rushing terror between Holly's ears.

Eli pulled up on the reins and brought his horse to a skidding halt. A gunshot?

He'd ridden right to the edge of Holly's property line. He wasn't but a mile from her house. Spurring Chester's side, Eli pushed the horse into an all-out run toward Holly's house.

Within a couple of minutes, he galloped into her yard to see her kneeling next to Sassy's side pressing gauze onto an area just above her front leg on the meaty part of her shoulder. Holly's mother stood on the porch speaking to someone on the other line.

Holly looked up, eyes blazing. "Someone's gone too far this time." Tears streaked her cheeks and her hands shook. He didn't know if it was from grief or rage.

Mrs. Maddox said, "Doc Gardner said he'd meet you at the office."

Eli pulled his cell phone from his pocket and placed a call to the sheriff's office. Within minutes, he had officers on the way. He slid his arms under Sassy and lifted her against his chest. "Let's get her to the vet. I've called Alex and he's sending Joel and Harlan. One will stay with your mother while the other one investigates."

Holly ran for her truck, returning within minutes. Duster whined and pranced about them.

Holly snapped her fingers and pointed to the house. "Stay."

Duster slunk off and Eli settled Sassy into the back of the truck. He climbed in and said, "I'll ride back here with her. You drive."

"You're sure?" Anxiety glittered in her eyes.

"I'm sure, Holly, let's go." If Sassy didn't make it, he didn't want the dog dying in her arms.

Thirty minutes later, Sassy lay on the table in the vet's office, X-rays finished. The doc removed his gloves and said, "I think she'll be fine. The bullet's entered her shoulder and the X-rays show that it didn't hit any bones. I'll get it out and she should be good as new in a few weeks."

Relief rolled over Holly's face and Eli felt his own neck muscles loosen a fraction. He wrapped an arm around Holly and gave her a squeeze.

Holly looked at the doctor. "I guess just call me and let me know how she's doing, will you?"

"You got it, darlin'. You know who shot her?"

Resolve hardened Holly's features. "No, but I'm going to find out."

Saying their goodbyes, they made their way from the room.

Eli looked at her. "You have any idea at all what's going on? And why someone's working so hard to get your attention?"

Lips pursed, she blew out a frustrated sigh. "I'm not sure, but I have my suspicions."

He took her arm and led her out into the lobby. "Care to share those with me?"

She rubbed her palms on her jeans. How much should she tell him? "I'm being hassled to sell my land to a company called Transcross."

"Right, I remember you saying something like that. You mother wants you to sell and you don't."

"Exactly. I think she's just trying to make me feel like i would be fine if I wanted to. The land's a lot of work," she admitted. "And even with Mr. Ryan's sporadic help, between the store and the land, it's time-consuming and exhausting But I love it. For now. Ask me again in a couple of years an I may feel different. I don't think so, but…" She shrugged.

"So these guys want you to sell out?"

"Yes, they want to build some kind of horse farm resort thingy." She waved a hand in disgust. "Apparently, our location on top of the mountain with the rolling hills, the view for miles, etcetera, is absolutely perfect and would bring in millions."

"Are they offering you a fair price?"

"Actually, yes, but it's not about the money. It's my home. I don't want to leave and I shouldn't be forced—or scared—into doing it." She looked at him. To tell or not? Uncertainty trembled inside her. She needed help. Taking a deep breath, she plunged on. "They threatened me. And my mother."

"What?" He looked outraged. "Why didn't you tell me?"

"They told me not to. At least I think it was them. I can't think of anyone else who would benefit from threatening me. The guy that grabbed me in front of the sheriff's office said that I should accept a generous offer, and that if I told anyone I was being harassed, my mother and I might end up with more medical bills, but I need help, Eli." Tears pricked then began a slow dribble down her cheeks. When he reached out a finger to catch one, the dam broke. "I simply can't do this alone anymore," Holly swiped at the tears, grateful for his support. Voice shaking, she said, "They don't play by the rules and I don't know how to fight dirty."

Distressed by her emotional outpouring, he pulled her into a tight hug. She let him, needing his comfort, his closeness. Then he said, "You think Transcross has something to do with everything that's happening?"

"Yes, but I don't know how to prove it."

Eli looked at his phone. Still no call from Ken. Tracing a plate was simple. He resolved to call Ken later if the man didn't get back to him soon.

His mind tripped over itself coming up with several plans of action. He rejected them all except one.

That evening, Holly spent her time at the church making sure all of the last-minute details were taken care of for the auction the next day. Once again, Alex dogged her steps, offering to carry something for her, bringing her a bottle of water. Nice things, just things she didn't want Alex to be doing.

Now, if Eli was the one...

But Eli had stayed home with his father because Buckey had some personal business to attend to with his daughter.

From the corner of her eye, she saw Alex heading her way again. She turned, bumped into a table and sent items flying.

"Here, let me."

Alex knelt next to her, grabbed a plastic bowl and lid and set it on the table.

"Thanks." Holly sidestepped him, but he was too quick. He snagged her hand.

"Well?"

She didn't have to ask what he meant.

He pressed. "What about tomorrow night?"

Holly swallowed. "No, thanks, Alex."

A sigh. "It's Eli, isn't it?"

"Yeah, kind of." She bit her lip, hoping he wouldn't be too mad. "But I don't even know if that's going to work out okay?"

To her surprise, he nodded. "Okay."

Okay? That was it?

He dropped her hand and walked away to start chatting with one of the other single ladies.

Shaking her head, she pushed Alex from her thoughts.

"I guess that's it," Mary said, coming up beside her.

Holly stretched the kinks from her back. "Yep. I think we're good to go."

Mary gave Holly a hug. "It's been fun doing this with you. I've enjoyed hanging out and getting to know you better."

Grinning, Holly returned the squeeze. "Absolutely. Speaking of hanging out and having fun, guilt hit her when she realized she still hadn't called Leigh-Ann.

And she still hadn't given Eli an answer to his letter.

Tomorrow was Valentine's. She really needed to get her act together.

Holly's cell phone rang. Glancing at the number, her heart flipped over. Eli. Climbing into her truck, she answered the call. "Hello?"

"Hey, Holly, do you have a few minutes?"

"I was just heading home, but sure."

"Do you want me to meet you somewhere? Are you hungry?"

"Starving." With everything going on, she'd skipped dinner. Now, it was pushing eight o'clock.

He laughed. "All right, see you in a few minutes at the diner on Main?"

"I'll be there."

Holly turned the key and the truck started right up. She let out the breath she didn't realize she'd been holding. Memories of the other night flooded back through her, causing her to shudder.

Glancing around, she realized Mary had already driven off. Once again, it was just her and the dark. Her stomach did another flip as she put the truck in Drive. Her eyes darting around the church parking lot, she didn't see any other cars. No headlights in front of her to blind her with the glare.

Nothing.

Her nerves eased and she headed down the mountain to the town below.

As she passed a small side road, she noticed a car approach the stop sign. Holly kept going and saw the car turn in behind her.

She tried to think who lived down that way. The Pastori family. And the Arringtons. Mr. Harvin who drove a truck for a food company.

The car behind her closed the gap and soon it was right on her tail.

Annoyance—and fear—hit her. Maybe it was just a teen being a pain. Or maybe it was whoever had been causing all of her other problems.

She pressed the gas and sped up a little. So did the car behind her. She flicked the rearview mirror so the headlights weren't in her eyes.

Just a couple more miles and she would hit the main street of town. Where Eli would be waiting. Grabbing her cell phone from the cup holder, she started to punch in Eli's number when she felt a harsh jolt from behind that jerked her forward against the seat belt then back against the seat.

Terror surged full force. "Hey!" she yelled, not caring there was no one to hear her. The headlights pulled closer and she braced herself for another hit.

When it came, the cell phone flew out of her hand to land on the passenger floorboard.

Fingers gripped the steering wheel in a white-knuckle grip. All she could do now was hang on and get to the bottom of the hill.

Or should she try to outrun him? Slow down? Find a turnoff?

Whispered prayers fluttered from her lips. *Please, God.*

He came at her again, this time hitting her hard enough to make her swerve to the edge of the mountain. She hit the guardrail and slid along it for a few feet. Sparks flew as metal screeched on metal.

Gritting her teeth to keep from screaming, she forced herself to keep a clear head, keep the fear and trembling under control.

Finally, Main Street came into sight. The car behind her made an abrupt turn and sped out of sight.

Holly braked to a halt in the middle of road. She sucked in gulps of oxygen and refused to cry. Her heart pounded in her throat and her head felt like it might explode.

The diner was right in front of her. Pressing the gas, she pulled forward into a parking spot.

Eli stepped out to meet her and got a glimpse of her truck. Eyes wide, he loped over to the driver's door. "What happened?"

"Someone just tried to run me off the road."

A vein in his forehead started pulsing. "What? Who?"

"I don't know who." She paused as she climbed out. "But I think it was the same one as the car that scared me in the parking lot of the church."

"What kind was it?"

"I got a glimpse of it in the streetlights this time. It was a large four-door car. Some type of sedan. A luxury car."

"Well, then," he said slowly, "my information might come in handy."

"What information?"

"That's what I wanted to talk to you about. I've been doing a little digging."

Seated at a booth across from him, Holly blinked at him. "What kind of digging?"

Eli pulled out a piece of paper where he'd written some things down. "I saw a car like the one you just described sitting outside your store the other day. I tried to approach them, but when they realized I was coming toward them, they drove away."

"Someone was watching my store?"

"Yeah. But I got the plate and called a buddy in New York to run it for me."

"Oh. And?"

"It's registered to a guy named Patrick Zimmerman."

"Zimmerman?" she nearly squeaked.

"Yeah, you recognize the name?"

"He works for Transcross."

Eli nodded. That was the information he had, too. "They're trying to force you off your land. If they destroy your business, they ruin your livelihood. If enough scary things happen, maybe you'll get scared and sell out."

"But that's ridiculous, I'm not selling no matter what they do."

He admired her spunk. Just one of the many things he

admired about her. "I know that and you know that, but I'm wondering if their tactics haven't worked before on someone else."

Holly shuddered. "So how do we stop them?"

"I've made a few calls and managed to get an investigation started." He leaned forward. "But until we get whoever's after you, you've got to take care, watch your back."

"I've been doing that. It's not working out so good for me." Her weak, yet brave, smile nearly did him in.

He grasped her hand. "I'm here for you, Holly, all right?"

She swallowed hard and nodded. "Thank you, Eli."

"Which brings me to another thing."

"What?"

"You never responded to my letter."

A light pink dusted her cheeks. "Oh, that."

"Uh-huh."

She studied him. He could almost see her thoughts. Take the leap? Or continue to be wary? A deep breath later, she smiled up at him. "I'd be honored to be your date tomorrow."

Relief, joy, gladness, all of those emotions and more flooded him. "I'm the one who's honored."

She gave a little laugh without a bit of humor in it. "That is if you don't mind dating someone who's a trouble magnet."

He tightened his fingers around hers. "I don't mind a bit. We're going to solve this together, all right?"

A small nod. He wasn't sure if that meant she believed him or not, but as far as he was concerned, he was back on cop duty until he was a hundred percent sure she was safe.

Holly stared into the mirror. Leigh-Ann and her mother stood behind her. "Well?"

"You're stunning."

"Thanks for the loan of the dress, Leigh-Ann. I waited until the last minute to even say I'd go to dinner with him so shopping wasn't even a possibility."

Black and red, the shin-length velvet hugged her trim form.

A high neck and long sleeves would ensure warmth. The matching black leggings and boots completed the ensemble.

"Not a problem." Her brown-eyed friend leaned over and hugged her. "Thanks for calling, I've missed you."

Holly smiled and stood. "I've missed you, too."

"I'm sorry I can't make the auction tonight. I forgot to ask for the night off and my supervisor put me on the schedule, so…" She shrugged. Leigh-Ann worked as a nurse in the Bryson City hospital.

"It's all right. Joel has to work tonight, too, doesn't he?"

"Yes, that's why I don't really mind going in. But I expect to hear all about it when we have lunch next week."

Holly hugged her. "You bet."

Thankfully, her mother seemed to be feeling better, although she said she didn't feel up to the chaos of the auction.

"Are you sure you'll be all right all by yourself?" Holly hated to leave her alone for too long. Mr. Ryan had volunteered to make a last minute pickup and deliver it to the auction so even he wouldn't be around.

"I'll be fine, Holly. I have a number of people I can call if I need to. Now get going."

A knock on the door sounded from downstairs and Holly's stomach did a nosedive. Then bounced back up. Rubbing her hands together, she said, "That's Eli."

The three women scurried from the room. Holly peeked out the window and gulped. He sent her blood pressure soaring and her heart into overdrive. However would she make it through dinner with him without babbling like an idiot?

"Holly, open the door." Her mother giggled like a schoolgirl. Holly's heart warmed at the sight.

She opened the door to see Eli decked out in dress pants and a collared shirt. A black wool blazer barely contained his shoulders. It was a good thing she'd taken a peek before opening the door. She wouldn't have been able to find her tongue.

"Hi there." He gave her a slow smile that set the butterflies in her stomach free.

She ignored them and grinned. "Hi."

He greeted Leigh-Ann and her mother, but never took his eyes off her. "You look stunning."

Giggles and laughter ruptured from behind her. She rolled her eyes then smiled. "Thanks, I'm glad everyone's in agreement tonight."

He offered his arm; her mother handed Holly her purse and practically shoved them out the door. The only thing that marred the leaving was the cop car sitting in her drive to keep an eye on her mother. A painful reminder that all was not right with her world.

But at least her mother would be safe.

Eli opened the door of his truck and helped her up and into the seat.

Once they were on the way, Holly said, "I hate to bring this up, but have you heard any more from your friend in New York?"

"Nothing yet. I'm sure he'll get back to me soon."

Twisting the strap of her purse, she watched the trees zip by. "I reported what happened last night on my way down the mountain."

"Good, at least it'll be on record."

"That's what I thought, too."

The conversation was stilted, her nerves tight. But she reveled in his presence. Could she really believe he was home for good?

"Are you really…"

"Holly, I promise…"

They'd spoken simultaneously. And just like that the ice was broken. He reached over to grasp her hand as they both laughed. "I don't want this to be awkward."

She took a deep breath. "I don't, either. We used to laugh so much, remember?"

"Yeah, I do. I want that back."

"Then let's get it back."

He grinned. "Deal."

The Steak House was located on the outskirts of town off a little road that looked like it went nowhere. However, the restaurant was well visited by locals and tourists alike.

Eli parked and Holly waited for Eli to come around and open the door for her. He did and took her hand to help her down from the truck. "You really do look beautiful."

His husky voice sent shivers along her nerve endings. "Thanks, Eli." She grinned. "You don't look so bad yourself."

They laughed and headed for the restaurant.

Two steps later, she stumbled to a stop. If Eli hadn't had a grip on her hand, she might have tripped and fallen.

Alex stood on the porch, drink in hand, staring at them as they approached. Taking a deep breath she said, "Hello, Alex."

NINE

"Holly, Eli."

Eli fingers had tightened almost painfully on hers. She wiggled them and he loosened his grip. "Alex."

Holly ignored Alex's unwavering stare as his eyes followed them into the restaurant. Eli leaned over next to her ear. "Do you want to go somewhere else?"

Anger spurred her. She thought Alex had moved on. Only now here he stood, watching her. "Absolutely not. Unfortunately, this is a small town and Alex Harwood lives in it. I'm bound to wind up at the same restaurant as he is upon occasion. Let's just go in and forget about him, okay?"

Admiration glinted. "Good for you."

Ten minutes later, they were seated in a booth. She said, "It's a good thing you made reservations. I think the whole town turned out here."

"I figured it would be like this."

Conversation flowed and Holly managed to relax and enjoy it in spite of the meeting with Alex. He must have decided to leave because she never saw him enter the place.

The steak had never tasted better and Holly didn't want the evening to end.

She took a sip of tea and leaned back to sigh. "I'm stuffed."

Eli set his fork on his plate. "I know the feeling." He nodded in the direction of Buckeye and his daughter. "They came in a little while ago."

Holly smiled at the man who waved back. Then his brow furrowed and he said something to his daughter who nodded. Buckeye rose and approached their table.

"Eli, I forgot to tell you, you had a phone call today from a Captain Longworth."

"Oh?"

"Yeah, said to tell you congratulations."

A sick look came over Eli's face and Holly wondered who this captain was.

Buckeye rubbed his chin. "Asked me to tell you that the decision about the position you interviewed for had been made and you got the job. Said he'd call you back with details, but wanted you to know."

Holly's heart splintered into a million tiny pieces. Eli would leave again. This time she knew she'd never be able to put her heart back together again.

Eli's eyes met hers and he opened his mouth to speak, but the shattering pain coursing through her didn't want to hear it. She shoved her chair back and grabbed her purse.

Without a word, she walked from the restaurant, eyes straight ahead refusing to let the tears fall. She heard him call her name, but knew she could be well on the way down the road and out of sight by the time he paid the bill and got in his truck.

Five minutes later, a car pulled up beside her and at first, fear flooded her, then she saw who it was.

"Holly?" her lawyer asked through the open window. "You need a ride?"

"Hi, Mr. Parker. Yes, that would be great. Thanks." Now let Eli find her and try to schmooze her with his numerous excuses. No, thanks. The tears threatened to rival the waterfall at the top of the mountain. Sheer willpower kept them at bay.

"Where are you headed?"

"Home."

"Are you okay?"

"Not really, but I don't want to talk about it if that's all right."

"Sure."

He fell silent and Holly watched the scenery roll by. How could she have been so stupid? But he'd seemed sincere. Had even talked about God like he knew Him.

Doubt hit her. Had she jumped to conclusions? Had it been fair to just leave without giving him a chance to explain? But memories of his past actions had assailed her in vivid detail. And the pain. Wow, had anything ever hurt that much? Very few things in her life had caused her that much pain. The death of her dad and her mother's cancer.

Eli's betrayal.

They passed the turnoff to her house. "Hey, Mr. Parker, you missed the turn."

"Oh, sorry."

He kept driving. Finally, she demanded, "What are you doing?"

The man sighed. "I'm taking you to meet someone."

"What?" she cried. "I don't want to meet with anyone. I want to go home!"

"Sorry, Holly, but some very important business needs to be taken care of and you have to be there."

Eli couldn't believe she'd just walked out him. He gunned the truck and searched the darkness. She couldn't have gone far. His cell phone rang and Eli snatched it, hoping it was Holly.

It was Ken, his buddy in New York. "Hey, thanks for getting back to me. What have you got for me?"

"Sorry it took so long. As soon as I sat down to run your plate, Captain came in and sent me off on a case. Anyway, I've got a company. The car is registered to Patrick Zimmerman."

"Right, I knew that. Got anything else?"

"He works for Transcross Realty. Real skinny kind of guy."

A thought struck him. "Who's the owner of Transcross Realty, anyway?"

"I thought you might want that information. Transcross is owned by two men. Alexander Harwood, Sr. and Patrick Zimmerman. They've gotten into the resort business and are busy buying up property all over the place. They really seem to be focusing on North Carolina."

"Harwood?"

"Yeah, why? You know the name?"

"I sure do."

Eli thanked Ken and hung up, his mind churning the information even as his eyes scanned the road for Holly. Worry hit him. Where could she be?

He tried her cell phone. It went straight to voice mail. Had she known he'd call and turned her phone off? Or had something else happened?

He called her house, hoping to get her mother. Voice mail picked up.

Now he really was concerned.

Alexander Harwood, Sr. was Alex's father. And the man was a co-owner with Transcross Realty. Transcross Realty wanted Holly's property.

His worry mounting by the minute, he called the sheriff's office and asked for Alex.

"He's not here, Eli," Alice said.

"Do you know how I can reach him? It's kind of an emergency."

"I can try him on his cell phone."

"Great."

"Hold on a minute. If he answers, I'll patch you through."

Within a minute Alice was back on the line. "He's not answering, which is really strange. He almost always answers his cell."

"Give me Joel, would you?"

"Sure, hold on again."

This time the next voice Eli heard was Joel's. "What can I do for you, Eli?"

"I think Holly may be in trouble."

"Holly? Again? What is it this time?"

"Can you track the sheriff's car? He's not answering his

cell phone and I'm thinking he may be in trouble, too." No sense in explaining he thought Alex might actually be the cause of Holly's problems.

"What? Well, sure, we've got GPS systems in all of the cars. Just because we're not big-city New York doesn't mean we're small-time technology."

"Good. I'm heading out to Holly's place just to check, but I need to know where Alex is. It's very important. Might even be life and death important."

A pause, then, "All right, if it's that crucial, give me a minute and I'll tell you where the car is."

"Thanks." Eli hung on and listened to dead air as he drove to Holly's house.

The cop car was gone.

Not good. He ran to the door and knocked. "Mrs. Maddox? Are you in there?"

No answer.

He peered in the nearest window. Nothing.

A nudge on his leg nearly made him jump out of his skin. "Duster."

Absently, Eli gave the canine's head a pat and looked around. Nothing seemed out of place. Except the police cruiser was gone. Foreboding chilled him.

Then Joel was back on the line. "I'm getting a signal from Alex's car. It looks like it's up near that cabin of his. I tried to raise him on the radio and his cell and got nothing. I'm going to call Harley and the two of us will head up that way, too."

"I'll meet you there."

When the lawyer pulled in front of the cabin owned by Alex Harwood, Holly's foreboding tripled. "What are you doing, Mr. Parker? Why does Alex want to meet with me?"

Through the leafless trees, she could see down into her sweeping backyard. She thought she could see Duster chasing something.

The man waved a hand. "Just go inside, will you?"

Holly sat back and crossed her arms. "No, I won't. Not until you tell me what's going on."

A frustrated groan escaped him. "Get out, now."

Her door opened. "Welcome to the party, Holly."

She swung her gaze around and up to see Alex leaning on the door. The faint sound of the waterfall rushed in the background. "Alex? Do you have some answers to all this craziness? I've practically been kidnapped. Now, what's going on?" she asked once again.

"Get inside."

"Look, I'm getting really tired of…" Alex grabbed her arm in a bruising grip. Holly cried out and stumbled in the direction he pushed her.

Holly grabbed the offended area on her arm and stared at Alex. Cold chips of ice stared back at her. Real fear hit her. He was deadly serious.

Behind him, she saw Duster stop and stare up the mountain. The he took off toward her. He'd heard her cry.

Swinging her gaze back to Alex, she stuffed down her fear. So, it had been him all along. "You were the one who was scaring me to death?"

He snorted. "Apparently I wasn't doing a very good job. You were supposed to come running to me for protection. You didn't, so I had to come up with a plan B."

Holly just stared at him. "What do you want from me?"

"Your land. Pure and simple. Developed right, it's worth millions." His eyes narrowed and she shivered. "If you had just agreed to keep dating, we could have been married by now and all this would never have had to happen."

"You're not my type," she spat.

His hand shot out and caught her across the jaw. So shocked, she couldn't even scream as the pain raced up the back of her neck and radiated from her cheek and jaw.

Oh, God, do something!

"Get her in here," he ordered the lawyer. Mr. Parker looked stunned at Alex's physical violence.

She decided she'd have to appeal to him for help. "Mr. Parker, come on, you've known me all my life. My mother trusts you…."

"Shut up." Alex grabbed her arm and shoved her once more. This time, she made it through the door. Duster burst in right after her to plant himself against her left leg.

She heard Alex mutter, but he didn't do anything to the dog. Then the sight of her mother lying on the sofa brought her to a screeching halt. All thought of her own pain left her. "Mom!"

She rushed to the woman's side and grabbed her hand.

"She's just resting comfortably."

Holly whirled, rage and terror battling it out inside her. "What did you do to her?" she demanded.

"She'll be fine. She was so nice when I stopped by to inquire about all of the strange things going on with you. Seems she didn't have a clue about them. When she invited me in for a cup of coffee to discuss the danger you were in, I told the officer on duty to take a break and sat down to chat with your mother."

"What drug did you use?"

"A couple of sleeping pills. I thought I might have to force them down her throat, but like I said, she was very obliging. Dropped them in her coffee when she turned to get the cream." Holly didn't think it was possible, but his eyes turned even colder. "She'll be fine as long as you follow directions."

Fury bubbled up inside her and she stared at his gun, wondering if she even had a chance to get it.

Then he laughed, obviously reading her thoughts. "Don't even think about it."

Turning back to her mother, Holly saw that she did indeed look like she was just in a peaceful deep sleep. Her chest rose and fell with each breath.

So, her mother would sleep through this and hopefully be back in her bed when she awoke, attributing her nap to recovering from chemo.

"What do you want me to do?" she asked in a low voice, even as her mind scrambled for a plan.

Alex snapped his fingers at the lawyer who stood cowering in the corner. "Give her the papers."

With a trembling hand, Jarrod Parker reached inside his coat and pulled out a handful of papers. He shoved them at Alex, then stepped back, eyes darting between Holly and Alex.

The sheriff slapped the papers and a pen down in front of her. "You did me a real favor running out on ole Eli tonight. I told Jarrod to get over there to that restaurant, get you alone and tell you your mother needed you ASAP. Now, sign them."

Sign away her land? Her home?

She looked at her mother and took a deep breath. If that's what it took to get her mom home safe, then…

Holly picked up the pen.

Duster settled at her feet, lifted his head and whined. She shushed him. "Am I at least getting paid for the land?"

"As soon as you sign, the money will be wired to your account." He grinned, a feral splitting of his lips. "All nice and legal-like."

Her mind clicked along. Did he really think she was that dumb? "And then you kill me and my mother, make it look like an accident that you'll investigate and get off scot-free. Not to mention get your money back somehow."

His chin jerked like she'd punched him and she saw the truth stamped on his face before he wiped it clean.

Alex took a deep breath and pulled his gun. "Sign the papers, Holly, or I'll blow her away right now."

Holly jumped up, pointed at Alex, and yelled, "Dust it up, boy!"

Duster bolted to his feet and planted himself on top of Alex, his big body knocking the man backward. She heard the gun land with a thump and Mr. Parker holler.

Holly scrambled for the gun, elbowing the lawyer in his chest. He fell back and she tripped when he grabbed her ankle, her fingers skimming the barrel of the weapon. Kicking out with her other foot, she caught the wrist of the hand that held her and with a cry of pain, he released her. Holly rolled to her feet and flew out the door while Duster still had Alex distracted.

She was hedging her bets that Alex wouldn't kill her mother until he had Holly back under his control. He needed the woman as leverage. Which meant she had to get away and stay out of his hands. Sheer terror shot through her, adrenaline pumping her legs toward the waterfall.

A gunshot rang out and she flinched, expecting to feel the piercing pain of a bullet entering her flesh.

She felt nothing so kept running, sending up desperate prayers for everyone's safety.

This was her one chance. She had no doubt that if Alex captured her again, she and her mother were dead.

Tripping and stumbling through the woods, her goal was the waterfall. She could hide there until Alex gave up.

Then she could go for help. She had to make it work. Her mother needed this to work.

Fear made her weak, but she pushed through it.

Another thought hit her. Alex couldn't let her escape no matter what. She knew too much. But her mother didn't.

If Holly died, the land would revert back to her mother.

And Alex would convince the woman to sign the papers. He'd use her grief against her and easily persuade her that selling was the best thing.

So that meant Alex would be shooting to kill.

Her death, investigated by him, could possibly be explained away by a stray bullet. Poachers she'd accidentally come across. Anything he came up with would be accepted because he was the sheriff.

But Eli knew.

Eli would investigate her death—until Alex killed him, too.

Eli. Oh how she wished she'd stayed and listened to him.

Duster shot ahead of her.

Oh, no, had the dog led Alex along her path? Surely, he'd run too fast for Alex to keep up.

Another shot rang out and a bullet kicked up the dirt in front of her.

Panting, gasping, she added what little extra burst she could to her feet and shot forward. Duster hit the cold water of the shallow part of the river that led to the waterfall. He yelped and scrambled out. Holly stopped at the edge and bent double at the stitch in her side. She stumbled to the edge of the river, desperate to catch her breath and keep going at the same time. She'd either have to cross the river or go down the side of the falls.

The water was too cold, she'd go into shock and suffer hypothermia. Backing away from the river, she knew it would have to be the side of the waterfall.

Just as she headed for the edge to climb down, something knocked against her and she hit the freezing water face-first.

TEN

Eli heard the second gunshot and fear for Holly grabbed his heart.

Joel was already at the cabin, climbing out of his car. Eli's window was down and Joel approached him, frowning. "I still can't get the sheriff on the line."

"I think Alex is the one behind all this. Don't let the man catch you off guard." Eli jumped out of the car, his gun in hand, ignoring Joel's shocked stare. Then he stopped, turned back. "I mean it, Joel, I have proof."

Joel's jaw clenched, he hesitated then nodded.

The door to the cabin stood open and Eli approached it with care. The shot had come from his left, but he had to check the interior of the building first.

Stepping in, he saw Jarrod Parker leaning over Holly's mother, who sat on the edge of the couch, rubbing her eyes.

"Freeze, Parker. Where's Holly?"

The man spun around and raised his hands when he saw Eli's gun. "I didn't know what he was going to do. It wasn't supposed to happen like this."

Joel stepped forward. "We'll figure that out later. Where's Alex and Holly?"

"I don't know. Holly sicced her dog on Alex and then ran out the door." The man's throat bobbed and sweat poured from his brow. "I didn't know what he was doing, I swear I didn't. I…I think he's going to kill her."

Eli bolted from the cabin yelling behind him, "I'm going after Holly. Get a doctor out here for Mrs. Maddox."

Not bothering to wait and see if his orders were followed, Eli took off, his feet pounding the hard earth. Absently, he registered the snow that had started to fall while he'd been in the cabin. Wind whipped around him, digging under his collar and stinging his neck. His eyes searched the ground and saw the scuffed earth heading in the direction of the trees.

Where would she go?

Distant barking reached his ears as did the sound of the rushing waterfall. Duster?

Gun held in front of him, Eli headed for the waterfall. A siren sounded behind him and when he looked back, he could see two other cruisers pulling up to the house.

Joel had Jarrod Parker cuffed.

Eli resumed his run toward the waterfall. Duster's barking increased in volume.

"Duster? Holly?" he yelled, not really expecting Holly to hear him.

Duster crashed from around a tree and yipped at him then took off back toward the falls.

Eli noted the dog's wet fur and spurred his feet to move faster over the uneven ground. He tripped once, caught himself and kept going.

Fear flooded him. Was Holly even still alive? He had to believe that. His heart wouldn't let him think otherwise. Had she fallen in the water?

Eyes roving, Eli took in everything, noting the freshly crunched path his feet now trod. Thankfully, the snow hadn't started earlier. Their trail would be completely covered in about thirty minutes.

They'd gone to the left. No doubt Holly trying to take cover in the woods. Hurrying, he made his way forward, to the sound of the river greeting his ears. The crashing falls were just up ahead.

And so were Holly and Alex.

Bursting into the clearing beside the water, he saw the two locked together in a struggle in the middle of the waist-deep river. Holly looked ready to lose at any moment.

Fortunately, the water didn't flow so fast that one couldn't stand up in it, but it was frigid cold and that meant almost more danger than possible drowning.

Forging a path in that direction, Eli yelled, "Let her go, Alex!"

The man either didn't hear him or ignored him.

Alex swung Holly to the side and shoved her under.

And held her.

Eli's heart dropped into his toes. "Alex!" The scream ripped from him and he trained his gun on the man's heart. Alex finally looked up and spotted Eli.

Fury and desperation flashed across his features and his grip must have loosened as Holly managed to get her head above water. Then Alex went down.

Holly had pulled his legs out from under him.

Good girl, Holly, keep fighting, honey. God, help me out here, please!

Eli hit the water running. The cold sucked the breath from him and nearly knocked him off his feet. But he had to get to Holly.

The water churned as it shoved Holly and Alex closer to the edge of the waterfall.

"Holly!"

She heard him and whirled. Her feet went out from under her again and for a few heart-stopping moments, Eli couldn't spot her. Then he saw Alex with a grip on her jacket. She slid out of it before he could get a better grip and slogged her way toward him. He could see her teeth chattering and her lips were blue. He had to get her out of the water now.

"Come on, Holly, you can do it."

Duster now stood on the banks of the river, barking nonstop.

"Eli!" she called and held her hands out toward him.

"Come on!"

Making his way toward her as fast as he could, he saw her strength ebbing.

And Alex's furious strides rapidly closed the distance between them.

Everything in her said to give up. She could hear Alex cursing behind her, the falls rushing just ahead and Eli shouting at her to come on.

Exhaustion pulled at her. She wanted to sink into it, let the water take her wherever it would.

But she couldn't. Her mother needed her. She wanted a future with Eli.

And she wanted justice.

She had to make it to Eli.

Please, God, help me.

Her legs gave out and she went down on one knee. The current tugged at her.

She let it swing her around to see Alex standing on a rock in the middle of the river, his gun aimed in her direction. Stupidly, she wondered if it would work after being submerged in the water.

Then she heard the crack.

Waited for the slam of the bullet.

Only it never came.

As though in slow motion, she watched Alex tumble from his rock and hit the water.

Then someone had her by the arms and her head bounced against a hard chest.

Nearly numb, she just wanted to sleep. Vaguely she wondered why she didn't feel cold anymore.

Just numb. She wanted to ask about her mother, but couldn't form the words.

Cold lips pressed against her forehead then everything faded to black.

* * *

Eli pulled Holly from the water. Worried about hypothermia, he knew they had to get her warmed up. He ignored the fact that he was shivering uncontrollably.

"Eli!"

Joel. The one who'd shot Alex. Keeping Holly next to him, he shouted, "I'm coming."

"Ambulance is here. I called it for Holly's mom, but managed to drag Alex's hide out of the water and they've got him, too. I've got another one on the way. By the time we get her back to the house, it should be here."

"We've got to get her warmed up. She's not even shivering anymore and her breathing seems shallow."

Eli felt his own legs tremble as he carried her, her beautiful black and red outfit now weighted down, dripping.

But he'd get her to the ambulance.

Fighting the fatigue and ignoring the chills racking him, he finally made it to the cabin.

Joel met him outside and said, "Mr. Parker made a full confession in hopes for a lighter sentence. Harlan took him on in. How's Holly?"

"Cold."

Mrs. Maddox, looking groggy but aware, got one look at her daughter and gave a small cry. "Holly."

"Can you get her in a warm shower?" he asked her mother.

She nodded, but before they could act, the third ambulance pulled in and Eli let the emergency personnel take over. Soon, they had Holly in the back of the vehicle wrapped in warm blankets, doing their best to get her body temperature up. Eli climbed in after her. Mrs. Maddox said she felt well enough to ride up front.

A paramedic started an IV of warm fluids. At Eli's raised brow, the female technician smiled. "When Joel called for another ambulance, he said something about being near the waterfall. We came prepared."

"Good job."

"Here." She opened a bin behind her and pulled out another blanket. "It's warm."

Eli took it and wrapped it around himself, but didn't think it was going to do much good. He was soaking wet and cold but much more concerned about the unconscious woman in front of him.

"How's her heart rate?"

Often people suffering from hypothermia went into cardiac arrest.

The paramedic listened. "Strong and steady. She's breathing better, too. Temp's creeping back up."

Eli felt relief flood him.

Thirty minutes later, they pulled into the hospital. Holly opened her eyes when the ambulance came to a stop.

"Eli? Mom?" Terror shot across her face. "Alex?"

He grabbed her hand. "Hey, your mom's fine. Alex is…in custody. And everything's going to be all right."

There was no more time to say anything as Holly was lowered from the ambulance and rushed into the emergency room.

Eli watched the door shut behind her, then he closed his eyes and breathed a prayer of thanks.

When Holly opened her eyes, she squinted against the brightness. "Turn the light off," she mumbled.

The bed shifted. Someone sat beside her. She sniffed. Eli. Her stomach flipped at his familiar scent. A scent she'd come to love.

"How's my mom?" she whispered.

Eli's deep voice rumbled to her. "The doctor said she was okay. You can see her a little later."

"And Alex?" She opened her eyes and looked up at him.

Eli dropped his gaze. "He died in the ambulance."

She sucked in a deep breath, feeling sadness for such a wasted life. "Oh."

Her eyelids felt so heavy. She closed them.

Eli spoke again. "Are you still with me?"

"Yeah. Just tired."

"Alex's dad was behind the whole mess involving you."

"The break-in at my store?"

He nodded. "Alex hired some punk from a neighboring town to throw a scare into you. Joel tracked him down. The kid didn't know who told him to do it, but phone records trace back to the pay phone near the sheriff's office so it's a pretty good bet it was Alex that made the call."

"And the men in the black car?"

"Already taken care of. Alex's dad hired them when he realized his son wasn't making any progress with you. One of them shot Sassy, too."

She grimaced. "He wanted my land. Alex said I should have just married him and none of this would have ever happened. On the one hand, he was doing everything he could to get me to fall in love with him. On the other, he was trying to scare me into running to him. That was him at my house, wasn't it? And in the car at the church?"

His hand rubbed her arm. It felt good. He said, "Yes. We think so. Apparently, Mr. Harwood, Sr. gave Alex an ultimatum. Get your land one way or another or get lost."

Her eyes fluttered open. "What? He did?"

"Yes. So Alex had to step up the incidents. He was trying to get you to run to him for protection."

"I ran to you instead."

Eli leaned over to kiss her lips. She reveled in the feeling until she remembered. She pushed him back. "The auction!"

"All taken care of. Mary and the rest of the committee stepped in and took over like champs."

Holly wilted back against the bed, lips still tingling from his kiss. Lifting a hand, she caressed his cheek. He needed to shave. "I'm so glad you came home when you did, that you were here for me during this horrid time."

"I'm so sorry I wasn't here before."

"It's all right. You're here now. And you kept Valentine's

Day from being quite a deadly day. I don't suppose I'll ever look at February foureenth the same again." She shivered and closed her eyes. Felt him lean in for another kiss.

"I love you, Holly Maddox. I've loved you for a long time, but now I know *how* to love you. Like Christ loves us. Unselfishly and unconditionally."

Tears flooded her eyes. "I love you, too, Eli. But you've got a new job, you're leaving again," she whispered.

He brushed the tears from her cheeks. "No, I'm not. You ran out before I had a chance to tell you that, yes, I had applied for the position some months ago, but then after my partner died and Dad got hurt and I came home…" He shrugged. "My priorities had changed. I forgot about the job. In fact, I just assumed they'd already filled it since it had been so long since the interview. But I don't want it. And I don't want to spend the rest of my life without you. I turned it down and accepted the job as interim sheriff of Rose Mountain, North Carolina. I plan to stay and help Dad at the farm and run for election in the next race for sheriff."

Speechless, Holly could only stare at him. "For real?"

He placed his lips on hers and her stomach flipped and quivered and she shivered all over again.

This time it didn't have anything at all to do with being cold.

She was very, very warm.

He smiled against her lips. "Yeah. For real. Happy Valentine's Day, darling."

She decided it wasn't such a bad day after all.

* * * * *

Dear Reader,

I hope you enjoyed Eli and Holly's story. I had a great time creating them and dropping them in the midst of trouble. When I was at the beach, I got a call from my agent saying Steeple Hill wanted me to be one of the authors in this anthology. Needless to say, I jumped at the chance. Right then, I grabbed my writing buddies and we brainstormed the whole story within about an hour. I just think it's so wonderful how God places people in our lives just when we need them. Eli arrived home in time to protect Holly and help figure out who was after her and her land. At first Holly wasn't real thrilled that he was there, but thank goodness God can see the big picture. Sometimes in real life, we don't always like or understand the way things work out, but one thing I've learned is that as long as I'm trusting God, He'll bring me through whatever storm crosses my path. Again, thank you for reading my story. I always love to hear from my readers. You can reach me at lynetteeason@lynetteeason.com.

God Bless!

Lynette Eason

QUESTIONS FOR DISCUSSION

1. At the beginning of the story, Holly is waffling between whether or not to give Alex another chance. Then her store is robbed and she sees Eli Brodie for the first time in months. Immediately, she knows she's not supposed to be with Alex. What makes her know this? Why does it take seeing Eli again to bring her to this conclusion?

2. What is your favorite scene in the book? Why?

3. Someone is after Holly's land and no amount of money interested her enough to sell. Do you have something that you value that much? (Not including living people like family or friends.) If so, what is it about that thing or place that means so much to you?

4. Holly is a worker, a go-getter. She's committed to her family, her home and her community. What did you admire most about her? Was there anything you didn't like about her?

5. Eli comes back to town a changed man. Or so he says. What do you think about the way he wants to start things back up with Holly? Did his actions back up his words?

6. Did the identity of the villain surprise you? Why or why not?

7. Holly was in danger, felt like her mother was in danger and didn't tell Eli about the threats. What would you have done in her place? Would you have told or continued on alone, trying to figure out what to do?

8. What do you think about the changes tragedy brings to people's lives? Eli lost a good partner and friend, but his death left Eli a changed man, a godly one. Have you ever experienced anything like this or know anyone who has? How did it affect your life?

Read on for a sneak preview of
KATIE'S REDEMPTION
by Patricia Davids,
the first book in the heartwarming new
BRIDES OF AMISH COUNTRY *series*
available in March 2010
from Steeple Hill Love Inspired.

When a pregnant formerly Amish woman
returns to her brother's house, seeking forgiveness
and a place to give birth to her child,
what she finds there isn't what she expected.

Please, God, don't let them send me away.

To give her child a home Katie Lantz would endure the angry tirade she expected from her brother. Through it all Malachi wouldn't be able to hide the gloating in his voice.

An unexpected tightening across her stomach made Katie suck in a quick breath. She'd been up since dawn, riding for hours on the jolting bus.

Her stomach tightened again. The pain deepened. Something wasn't right. This was more than fatigue. It was labor.

Breathing hard, she peered through the blowing snow. It wasn't much farther to her brother's farm. Closing her eyes, she gathered her strength.

One foot in front of the other. The only way to finish a journey is to start it.

She sagged with relief when her hand closed over the railing. She was home.

Home. The word echoed inside her mind, bringing with it unhappy memories that pushed aside her relief. Raising her fist, she knocked at the front door. Then she bowed her head and closed her eyes, grasping the collar of her coat to keep the chill at bay.

When the door finally opened, she looked up to meet her brother's gaze.

Katie sucked in a breath and then took a half step back. A tall, broad-shouldered Amish man stood in front of her with a kerosene lamp in his hand and a faintly puzzled expression on his handsome face.

It wasn't Malachi.

To read more of Katie's story,
pick up KATIE'S REDEMPTION
by Patricia Davids, available March 2010.

Love Inspired®

After two years away, Katie Lantz returns to her Amish community nine months pregnant—and unmarried. Afraid she'll be shunned, she's shocked to meet carpenter Elam Sutter, who now owns her family farm. Elam and his kindly mother show Katie just what family, faith and acceptance truly mean.

BRIDES OF
Amish Country

Look for

Katie's Redemption

by

Patricia Davids

Available March wherever books are sold.

www.SteepleHill.com

From two bestselling authors comes this volume
containing two heartwarming Easter stories that
celebrate the renewal of love, life and faith.

Easter Promises
by
Lois Richer and Allie Pleiter

Available March wherever books are sold.

LARGER-PRINT BOOKS!

**GET 2 FREE
LARGER-PRINT NOVELS
PLUS 2 FREE
MYSTERY GIFTS**

Love Inspired®
SUSPENSE
RIVETING INSPIRATIONAL ROMANCE

Larger-print novels are now available...

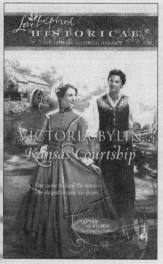

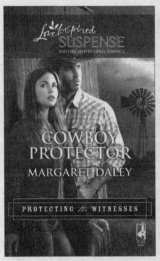